NOBODY DOES IT BETTER

LAUREN BLAKELY

HIS PROLOGUE

Shaw

Some women are just forbidden. Like . . . oh, just off the top of my head . . . say, my sister's lifelong best friend. Forbidden, as in if I touch her, it's sayonara favorite-body-part.

Do I kid?

No, and I don't want to test my sister's resolve, so I stay far, far away from lovely Vanessa. Sweet Vanessa. Vanessa who wants the real deal. *Keep your dirty hands off my best friend* Vanessa.

Hey, that's what my sister said.

Look, I'm not scared of my sister.

But I do respect her. I was raised right. I was taught respect, honor, and duty. And above all . . .

family comes first. When Perri told me years ago she'd have my balls in a sling if I put my ladies'-man paws anywhere near her bestie, I listened, because I happen to like the boys a helluva lot.

Honestly, though, I followed her guidelines not just for the sake of my intact nuts. I did it because she *asked*. If it's important to Perri that my dirty hands stay far, far away from Vanessa, I can abide by that.

I can resist sexy, alluring, flirty Vanessa.

Witty, clever, *oh, look, there's mistletoe above us* Vanessa.

Oh, did I say that?

Well, Vanessa did, and I'll never forget that Christmas party when we were home from college.

But I swear, it was only a kiss. A sweet, tantalizing, drive-my-body-insane-with-wanting-more kiss. I've *mostly* stayed away, and that's not been easy, so give a man some points for stellar restraint.

Especially since I've had it bad for Vanessa for years.

As in decades.

But sometimes, over the decades, you slip a little bit when you want something. You bend to the left, to the right, and you steal another kiss. Fine, fine. There was *one* more time—a year ago, when we were at Vanessa's bowling alley for a New Year's Eve party, lifting glasses and toasting to the new year.

It wasn't like we got it on right there on the bowling ball return.

(It was beside the dartboard.)

And it was a chaste New Year's kiss.

Too chaste for me.

When I was home alone in bed, though, nothing was innocent that night. In my mind, it was one hot, sexy, filthy kiss that made us both rip off clothes.

Except, even then, those words—*balls in a sling*—echoed.

I listened. I'll keep listening. After all, it's only lust I feel, right?

I can set that aside, no problem.

Until the weekend before my sister's wedding . . .

HER PROLOGUE

Vanessa

Is there any sadder adjective to describe a man you're jonesing for than *off-limits*?

Okay, fine. There might be a few worse qualities in a guy, like woefully dumb, boring AF, and, say, rude to his mama.

Also, dislikes dogs.

For the record, no dog-disliker is getting under my skirt.

But let's say you really dig a guy. The last thing you want is for him to be unavailable.

That's the trouble with Shaw. That's always been the trouble with him, ever since I crushed hard on the guy way back in seventh grade.

I fell for him because he cracked me up.

Like that time in history class, when we were studying the English monarchy and he raised his hand and asked in an intensely curious voice, "Excuse me, Mr. Wabash. Which king of England invented fractions?"

Mr. Wabash turned from the board, his white chalk suspended mid-stroke, his brow furrowed, and said, "I'm not sure that was a king of England."

Shaw leaned back in his chair, a naughty grin creeping across his thirteen-year-old face, and coolly quipped, "It was Henry the Fourth."

I chuckled.

Maybe I laughed loudly.

Fine, I snorted.

We were both sent to the school office, where he proceeded to fire off round after round of jokes in a murmur as we waited side by side for the principal.

How did the Vikings send secret messages?

By Norse code.

Why should you never trust an atom?

Because they make everything up.

They were corny jokes, but hey, that was comedy gold in seventh grade.

The principal called us into his chambers and folded his hands the way annoyed adults do. He reprimanded Shaw for disturbing the class and rebuked me for laughing too loud.

He sent us back to class with a warning.

I was so glad Shaw was only eleven months older than his sister, putting the three of us in the same grade in school.

He kept up his cute jester routine all through high school, during college when he became more of a sexy jester to me, and even now, as I'm pushing thirty. Like when he juggled five rawhide bones at his parents' house a few months ago. Their dog was quite taken with his skills.

Or when he performed a comedy act at the fireman talent show last year. Though, in all honesty, I spent most of his routine focusing on his V line rather than his punch line.

He was shirtless. I had no choice.

Big surprise that somewhere along the way, I fell for him.

For his humor, for his heart, and for his big, strong body.

That's the problem.

He's fall-for-able, and I'm not the only woman who's noticed.

The ladies love him, and he seems to love them too.

So, stolen kiss or two aside, I simply can't think about him any longer.

For many reasons, but first and foremost, this—he's my best friend Perri's brother. She's never said it to me, but I *know* she doesn't want me with him. And I hate keeping secrets from her.

I must be done with this years-in-the-making secret.

So when I have the chance to meet a new guy who's coming back to town, a man who's simply perfect for me, I seize the opportunity.

So what if there are nearly two decades of longing for my best friend's brother to get over?

1
VANESSA

I have this fantasy.

The details vary a little. Sometimes I'm in the town diner, other times I'm walking across the square. Most of the time, I'm right here at the one-stop check-in and shoe counter at my bowling alley.

The rest of it goes like this: This guy strides up to me. A rush of tingles spreads down my chest at the sight of his dark hair, his five-o'clock shadow, and his big, burly frame. He drums his fingers on the Formica, lifts a brow, then smiles.

I mean one of those world-class, panty-melting grins that make you swoon.

But the real swoon is what comes next.

He'll say, "Level with me, Vanessa. I've had it bad for you for most of the last two decades, and I'll wager it's the same for you. If you feel even one ounce of what I feel, let's shed this whole ruse and make it official. Go out with me. Go out with me tonight."

The rest? It's a montage of *oh yeses;* hot, wet kisses; and messy lipstick.

That's the fantasy. My *reality* on a Wednesday evening in February?

The door opens and a familiar figure strolls in. Even from a distance, he catches my gaze then tips his chin and mouths *hey*.

My stomach flips, and then it somersaults again when he reaches my post, winks, and asks for a pair of shoes. I know his size, so I hand him the fourteens.

"You know what they say about big shoes?" His deep, raspy voice makes my chest flutter.

I quirk up my lips. "That they're perfect for clowns?"

And that smile? Oh boy. It spreads into the sexiest grin. "Vanessa Maria Marquez, are you saying I'm a clown?"

I shrug, a little playfully, looking at the shoes in his hands. "If the shoe fits . . ."

He leans closer. "The other thing they say about big shoes is that it's *hard* . . ."

I wait for him to make a dirty joke, to lob an innuendo. Breath held, I wait for him to say *Let's do this*, because hope never dies. And then I wait for the abject guilt of keeping a secret from Perri to subside.

Perri, one of my two best friends in the universe, the girl who's been there for me through every up and down, who attended the theatrical productions I worked on in high school, the friend who rushed to my side in the hospital room when I broke my leg skiing in college, even though she was two hours away, the woman I gave the kick in the pants to last year with her guy when she needed it.

Shaw's hazel eyes flicker, and I know he's waiting for me to set up his dirty joke.

My guilt hardens—and my hope deepens too. The longing for this man beats on.

I return to his "hard" comment. "Hard for what?"

"Hard to find socks."

I laugh, shake my head, and shoo him off. "Go bowl some strikes, Shaw."

He gives me a tip of the imaginary hat and heads off to lane twenty, joining a few fellow firemen. I do my damnedest not to stare at his sexy butt, or admire his big frame, or, honestly, even think about him like that.

It's something I've been trying to do for years.

When a group of older ladies—twice my age and totally fabulous—comes in, I shift my focus, setting them up at one of the lanes and serving them wine.

For the next thirty minutes, I don't even look at lane twenty.

Well, maybe I peek once or twice.

2

VANESSA

Doris Day had it right.

Whatever will be will be.

The future is coming at you, so you just damn well better make the most of your present.

That's why I dress the way I do, listen to great tunes, and spend plenty of my days and nights here at Pin-Up Lanes, where I'm living the American dream.

I love bowling, I love retro clothes, and I love people.

So this suits me fabulously, thank you, Doris Day.

As her soulful number pipes through the place later that evening, I carry a tray of chardonnay-filled wineglasses past my cartoonish *Let's go bowling, it's great for a date* sign, and head straight for the vintage scoreboard.

I don't glance at lane twenty.

Instead, I deposit the tray at the ladies' table, set a hand on my hip, and shoot Miriam a playful look, tapping the toe of my Mary Janes. "You do know that to bowl, you have to send the ball down the lane." I sweep my arm toward the very empty lane that Chanel-No.-5-scented Miriam and her two friends are not using since they're gabbing. Which is fine by me. I'm also a gabber, and I love to gab with my besties too, whatever chance I get.

Miriam laughs—a rumbly, rich kind that matches her presence as the leader of the group. "Then we'd have to take a break from discussing Sara's new coconut-cake-baking skills."

The women break out in peals of laughter. They usually assemble for a book club at my friend Arden's store, but tonight they brought the book club here.

Narrowing my eyes, I tap a finger against my lip. "Hmm. Something tells me coconut cake is a euphemism. I wonder."

From behind her cat eye glasses, Sara lifts a brow as she grabs a glass of the wine. "Not true. I *did* make a coconut cake after I read this book." She grabs a paperback from the green-and-white plastic bench seats, slapping a dog-eared *The Coincidence of Coconut Cake* against her thigh. "Then, my boyfriend and I wanted to see if it was true what they say about coconut."

Miriam arches a brow. "Coconut?"

Sara's pure deadpan when she answers. "That it makes certain substances taste better."

Chuckling, Miriam shakes her head. "Honey, that's pineapple."

Sara wiggles her brows. "No, coconut does the trick too."

From her spot on the bench, CarolAnn adjusts her messy bun, shaking her head while laughing. "Ladies, if you don't watch your euphemisms, we're going to get kicked out of Pin-Up Lanes."

I wave a hand dismissively. "As if I'd ever kick you out for exchanging such useful intel." I smile then wave toward my usual post behind the counter. "On that note, I'll leave you to your *cake* talk. And feel free to not bowl one bit."

As I leave, CarolAnn calls out, "Vanessa, I love your dress, and I'm jealous you have the figure to pull it off. But not jealous enough to lay off the wine."

I swivel around, briefly glancing down at my swingy teal-blue number with a cherry pattern. "Wine is never the problem, and you're stunning. You'd look amazing in a cherry-pattern dress, and you absolutely have the figure for it. I'll take you shopping to prove it."

"Wait! I want to go shopping with Vanessa," Sara calls out.

Miriam's voice cuts through. "Evidently, you old birds are not above begging this sweet gal to take you shopping. It's like I can't take you out in public."

I laugh and leave the conversation with a wave, heading back behind the counter, where I busy myself checking in a few new bowlers. As I hand shoes to a family of four, I *don't* check out Shaw. Yay me. I deserve bonus points tonight.

A little later, Sara beckons me over to their lane with a wiggle of her fingers. "Vanessa, tell me something." Her cheeks are flushed, and she's bolder than usual.

"What do you want to know?"

"Are you still single?"

I shoot her a fierce stare for an answer, then I give her a verbal one. "Am I stealing whatever coconut cake you don't finish tonight? Is wine the greatest beverage ever? Does fashion rule? Yes, yes, yes, I am single."

Miriam grabs her phone, tapping quickly on the screen, while Sara takes the reins, answering me with, "Good, because we have someone in mind."

"Who would that be?" I'm not opposed to being set up. I'm open to meeting the right man, whether he's on an app, knows one of my friends, or is strolling down the street. And these book club ladies not only know men, but they've raised boys who've become men.

Miriam jumps in. "My stepson. He's a catch. You know him, I believe, since he grew up here. Jamie Sullivan."

My eyes widen. "Of course. Jamie Sullivan, as in two years older, captain of the football team, student athlete and valedictorian who went to Yale Law School?"

Miriam beams proudly. "He's the one."

My brow knits as I try to remember what I'd last heard about him. "But I thought he was involved?"

Her smile morphs into a satisfied grin. "Not any longer, and thank the Lord. I never did care for her, and she never seemed to care for him."

"I'm sorry to hear that."

Miriam tuts. "It's all for the best. I'm glad he figured it out before he proposed. But now he's single and ready to mingle . . ."

Her phone trills.

Miriam's eyes flicker with surprise. "Who could that be?"

Sara chuckles as the phone rings again. "Mir, you don't need to pretend. The jig is up."

Miriam grabs her mobile but keeps up the ruse. "Oh, look at that. He's calling." She answers her phone on a video call. "Hey, sweetie."

"Hi, Miriam."

"Jamie, it's so funny that you called."

There's a pause, and then he says in a smooth, masculine voice, "It's funny? You texted me and asked me to call. You used all caps. '*CALL ME IN EXACTLY FIVE MINUTES IF I SEND YOU A TEXT WITH A MONKEY FACE EMOJI.*'"

I snicker, and Miriam acts perplexed. "I don't think I said that, but be that as it may—want to hear the most coincidental thing?"

"Sure," he says, as Miriam adjusts the screen, showing me . . . oh my.

Jamie is even more handsome than I remember. He's aged well, and his dark-blond hair curls at the ends. Warm amber eyes meet mine, and his square jaw could be the factory model for square jaws. Full lips complete the handsome-as-*GQ* look. No wonder my little sister, Ella, had a crush on him when she was in eighth grade and he was a senior. I wave at his face on the screen. "Hi, Jamie. How are you?"

"Hey, Vanessa. How the hell are you? And, most important, has my stepmom enlisted you in some crazy scheme?"

I shrug lightly. "I'm fabulous, thanks for asking. As for your stepmom, I guess you'll have to ask her if she's meddlesome," I answer playfully.

Miriam beams, tossing a glance at her comrades-in-setup. "Look, they get along so well already."

Sara laughs. "You're forcing them to."

But she's truly not, because Jamie and I chat for a few minutes, catching up on the goings-on in our little town of Lucky Falls. He says he's practicing law in San Francisco, and I tell him I'm keeping busy here at the bowling alley.

"Are you still an avid theater-goer?" he asks, and I can't help but smile that he remembers a small detail about me from high school.

"I get to San Francisco as often as I can to see shows. My sister and I saw *Waitress* a few months ago. It was fantastic."

"Good to hear. How's Ella?"

"Keeping the library busy as always," I say, picturing my younger sister, the quintessential sexy and smart librarian.

As a new group of customers heads into the alley, I tell him it was nice chatting, but I have to go.

Once I've checked the newcomers in, Miriam strides over, a determined look in her gray eyes. "Look, I'm not going to pretend here."

I didn't think she was pretending before. "Good. Be real," I say with a smile.

She eyes me up and down. "You're lovely, fun, and pretty. Clever and kind too. So is Jamie. He's whip smart, sweet as can be, and reliable as anything. He's ready to settle down. You are too."

I'm taken aback by her bold assessment of my relationship readiness. "Why do you say that?"

Miriam points to my dark-brown irises. "You have that look. You're ready for the real deal. My son is the real deal."

"Is that so?" I ask, but I'm momentarily distracted because Shaw's heading in my direction, and he's wearing *that* grin.

That damn grin that gets me every time.

He slides up next to Miriam. "Hey, Miriam. How's everything at the library? You still volunteering and reading to the school kids?"

She flashes a smile. "Why, yes, I am."

"I bet they adore you. I know they loved you when you were teaching a few years back."

"And I loved teaching second grade up until the day I retired. The kids always got a kick out of it when the firemen visited the school."

"We're doing that next week, as a matter of fact." Then he nods at me. "Anyway, I'll let you two ladies finish up. Just wanted to say hello." He meets my gaze. "By the way, nice cherries."

My gaze drifts momentarily to the cherry pattern, and that fluttery hope springs up once more, wishing he'd say *Nice cherries. Want to go out for cherry pie?*

I don't even care for pie.

But I'd say yes.

Instead, he walks away.

He's always walking away.

In eight years of running this joint, I've always

hoped he'd walk back to me. But that's never happened.

That never will happen.

And I suppose it's truly for the best. I can't keep feeling this way for Perri's brother.

Maybe tonight is a sign it's time for me to move on from this best-kept secret.

I return my focus to Miriam, who's patiently waiting. Shaw's well out of earshot.

"That sounds great. Set me up with him," I tell her.

She punches the air, and I take a deep breath.

Miriam is correct. But that's another reason Shaw isn't right for me—he's a ladies' man, and I'm ready for the real deal.

* * *

Some decisions require best friend approval, even retroactively.

After I say goodbye to the last patron, a woman in a satin Pink Ladies jacket toting a matching bowling ball bag, I lock the door to Pin-Up Lanes.

Now it's just Arden, Perri, and me, since they arrived a few minutes ago, bearing wine. They've been my best friends since I moved to the United States from Colombia when I was six.

"You know I love you, but I love you more when

you arrive with a Syrah," I say as I grab a corkscrew, glasses, and some forks.

Arden winks. "We know you so well."

We park ourselves at the book club ladies' table, and I brandish the last slice of coconut cake they left for me. "Cake and wine time. Plus, it's special cake."

Tucking a strand of blonde hair over her ear, Arden asks, "Is it spiked?"

"Apparently, it makes everything taste better," I tell her in a deliberately sultry voice.

"Ooh la la." Arden laughs.

"I'll just sit here enjoying my olives," Perri says, presenting a small Tupperware container with her favorite salty green treats. She opens the bottle of wine and pours. "What are we toasting tonight? To spiked cake? Tasty, naughty things? Something else?"

I raise a glass. "To generally being awesome?"

She flashes a bright, big smile, her green eyes sparkling. "We are always awesome, so that is an excellent toast."

Arden clears her throat. "Hello? How about we drink to the two-week countdown?"

I lift my glass higher and stare pointedly at Perri. "To you walking down the aisle in two more weeks."

Arden joins in. "Yes, I am ridiculously excited. Winter Wonderland wedding, here we come."

Perri smiles, something she does a lot when we talk about her wedding, the happy bitch. "Let's hope the gods of snow dump at least three feet on Sugar Bowl," she says, since she and Derek will spend their honeymoon days skiing down that mountain and their nights climbing, well, other mountains, I'm sure.

We clink glasses and catch up on wedding details as we drink and devour the cake and olives. I've got the honeymoon lodging handled. Next week I'm going up to my grandparents' cabin at Sugar Bowl to make sure it's ready for the lovebirds. I assure them my granddad will meet me there to help me, and then I segue to the critical issue.

I glance at each of them. "All right, kickass girls of Lucky Falls, what do you think about Jamie Sullivan?"

Arden's brown eyes spark with curiosity. "As in the former prom king?"

I smile. "Jamie was quite a catch back in the day, wasn't he? Seems he is now too. His stepmother wants to set me up with him. We actually had a video call for a few minutes earlier."

"He's great," Perri says, jumping in. "Derek and I had dinner with him a few weeks ago, and I should arrest myself for not even thinking about setting you up with him." She holds out her wrists as if for cuffing.

I chide her. "Well, really. My single-tude should

be your foremost thought and not, you know, your pending wedding."

"But seriously, I can't believe I didn't think of it," Perri says, shaking her head.

"Why were you having dinner with Jamie Sullivan?" Arden asks.

"Derek's sister and her husband are good friends with him. He's a great guy. Friendly and funny—"

Perri stops.

Just freezes mid-sentence.

"What's wrong?" I make a *keep rolling* motion to get her to fill in the missing details. "He's friendly, funny, and *frumpy*?"

Arden laughs. "That's where your mind went?"

"It was alliterative. As a book shop owner, I thought you'd appreciate that."

"How about he's friendly, funny, and foxy? Maybe that's a better one."

I hum then concede her point as Perri recovers the power of speech, blurting out, "He's friendly, funny, and coming to my wedding! You guys can get together then!"

I smile and take a drink.

And I like that idea for a lot of reasons. There's only one fly in the ointment. "But don't you think I should make sure Ella doesn't mind?"

Arden blinks. "Why would your sister mind?"

"She crushed on him back in eighth grade," I

explain, grabbing my phone to tap out a text to my little sister.

Vanessa: Question: do you care if I go on a date with Jamie Sullivan?

Arden's brows knit together as I show her the text. "Isn't there a statute of limitations on crushes and claiming them?"

"I'm sure there is, but it's still best to ask first, don't you think?"

"And I bet Ella will be fine with it," Perri says. "C'mon, the three of us taught her everything she knows about boys."

Arden nods. "We done raised that girl right when it comes to appreciation of the male form."

A few seconds later, my phone buzzes with a reply, and since I lapse into my accent with Ella in person, I always seem to hear her texts that way too.

Ella: He is HAWT.

Ella: And smart.
Ella: And, wait for it, NICE.

Vanessa: So that's a keep-my-mitts-off-him warning, then?

Ella: Please. If someone is going to snag him, it might as well be a Marquez sister.

Vanessa: Love that sharing spirit.

Ella: You did teach me that sharing is caring. :)

Vanessa: So Jamie is on- rather than off-limits?

Ella: I'll leave you with this. Gurrrrl. Get on that, stat.

I show the screen to my friends.

"And now you have no reason not to go with him to my wedding," Perri says.

"I suppose I don't."

Though, truth be told, the biggest factor right now is that going with Jamie will keep my mind off how sexy Perri's brother will look in his groomsman tux.

And that's what I need more than anything.

3
BOOK CLUB LADIES GROUP CHAT

Miriam: I think that went swimmingly well! I'm rather proud of us. Especially moi. I was so smooth!

CarolAnn: Yes. Like ice. It was almost as if they had absolutely no clue what you were up to.

Sara: It was amazing how you made it seem sooo natural.

Miriam: Gee, thanks for nothing. Personally, I think we pulled off making it look spontaneous and not like something we'd been planning for several months.

CarolAnn: *arches skeptical brow* Only several months? I'd say you've had this on your mind for a few years. I'm just amazed that it took this long. And even with all that time to play, you still made it seem patently obvious.

Sara: We're going to need to send her back to acting school, CarolAnn.

CarolAnn: Signing her up now . . .

Miriam: Ha! You'll all be coming to me soon, wanting me to set up your sons, daughters, nephews, nieces, cousins . . .

CarolAnn: *sifts through list of young single people*

Sara: *hopes Miriam is right*

Miriam: All kidding aside, she seemed completely open to it. This is going to be good for everyone involved, don't you think?

CarolAnn: I do have to agree with you there. It feels like it was meant to be.

Sara: And we're going to make sure what's meant to be actually comes to be.

4

SHAW

Damn.

I check out my reflection in the mirror at the tux shop, shaking my head in over-the-top admiration. "I'd say it's amazing . . . but honestly, it shouldn't be a surprise I look good in anything. Formal wear was made for me."

Derek adjusts the lapels on his tux as he scoffs. "Hey, Shaw. Have you been tested lately?"

"For extreme levels of good-looking? Why, yes. I was off the charts."

"No, for your myopia, as in short-sightedness."

Gabe mimes banging a drum. "Boom."

"Oh, please. You're all just jelly I'm still single." I joke, since I know they're nothing of the sort. These two cats are most happily taken.

"Ha. As if I want to be out there hunting with the

likes of you." Gabe points at himself, his platinum band shining brightly under the fluorescent lights of the store. "Married, and happy as the happiest clam in the sea, thank you very much."

As a man should fucking well be when he's spoken for. And since Gabe is my closest bud, and Derek's become a damn good friend, I couldn't be more thrilled one of them has successfully tied the knot and the other will in one more week.

And yet, I also *must* razz them. "Then you're green with envy that I look this stunning. Damn, I should be the star of the firemen calendar." I smack my forehead. "Oh wait, I am. And clearly no one has ever looked as good in turnouts or a tux as I do."

Gabe clears his throat. "Don't worry. I'll keep your dirty little secret."

I lift a curious eyebrow. "What's that?"

"That you paid the calendar organizer for your placement on the cover."

Derek's eyes widen, and he chuckles under his breath. "Oh, I can't wait to spread that rumor."

Gabe straightens his bow tie. "It's no rumor. It's the God's honest truth."

"Like I said, jealousy is your color, Gabe," I toss back. Then I angle my head to nod at Derek, who's finishing up his final tux fitting, and drop the ribbing for a moment. "All kidding aside ... looking good."

He nods at my reflection, gratitude in the set of his jaw. "Thanks, man."

And because I'm not a dick, even though I love to give these guys a hard time, I narrow my eyes at the three of us in the mirror. "I mean, hell. Just look at us in our tuxes. We could be the models for this shop."

From behind me, the faint chuckling of the shop owner carries across the small store.

"Mr. Grayson," I call, "I know you're eager to slap our photo on the front window. Just admit it, and for you, we'll even do it for free."

"Thanks, but I don't want to scare anyone away," the older man deadpans as he ambles over and straightens the shoulders on Gabe's jacket.

I pout. "My modeling career is over. Guess I'll stick to my day job. Also, speaking of how good we look, allow me to say this." I turn and meet Derek's dark eyes then pat his shoulder, bro-style. "I'm glad my sister is marrying you."

Gabe places a hand on his heart. "Aww. I love it when Shaw goes all honest and mushy."

I glare at my friend. "I'm not mushy."

Gabe pinches his thumb and forefinger together. "A little mushy?"

I point at Derek. "He's a good guy. He treats Perri well. Nuff said."

"I do treat her well. She deserves nothing less." Derek's tone is heartfelt, full of the devotion he's displayed to my sister, and I'm so damn glad she found a man like him. "I'm a lucky guy," he tells me. "And I'm also glad you didn't pull any of that *don't touch my sister* shit."

I laugh. "Perri does that enough for all of us when she pulls her *don't touch my friend* shit."

Derek chuckles. "I've never met a lioness more protective of her sister lions."

I huff, wishing she wasn't that way, but what can I do?

I sidestep the issue, glancing at the silver-haired shop owner. "Hey, Mr. Grayson, I think I could work in a tuxedo shop. Want to know why?"

"Why's that?"

I wiggle my brows. "It suits me."

"Ugh," Derek groans, and Gabe joins in, followed by the proprietor. "Dude, you have the worst jokes."

"That's not true. I have awesome jokes. The ladies love them."

Gabe shakes his head. "I don't think they're laughing at your jokes. I think they just feel sorry for you."

I hold my arms out wide. "Who could feel sorry for me? Especially when they hear this one: what's the difference between a man wearing pajamas on a bicycle and a guy wearing a tuxedo on a unicycle?"

"What is it?" Derek asks.

"Attire," I say.

Gabe rolls his eyes. "You're killing us."

Mr. Grayson shoots me the side-eye. "If you keep this up, kid, you're not going to have any lady to escort down the aisle at this wedding."

"Please. They'll be lined up. Speaking of . . ." I turn to Derek. "Which fine bridesmaid will I be walking down the aisle?"

The groom casts a glance at Gabe, almost as if they're in on something, then answers, "Vanessa."

I can't even be bothered to wipe a little bit of the grin off my face. I was hoping that was what he'd say. "Excellent."

"But don't get too excited, because I don't think she's walking anywhere with you after that." Derek unknots the bow tie.

"Why's that?"

"It seems she's being matched with a date at the wedding," he says, all cool and casual as if this intel is no big deal, when it's a gargantuan mess of a cat's hairball.

I freeze. "Say that again."

"You know Jamie Sullivan, right? I think you went to high school with him." Derek shrugs out of his jacket and catches Mr. Grayson's gaze. "The tux fits great, sir."

"It sure does," the man says as he fiddles with Gabe's black jacket.

"Wait. What's the story with Jamie Sullivan?" I

ask crisply, remembering the all-American guy the girls in school fawned over.

Gabe taps his chin. "He was a few years older than you, wasn't he? And if memory serves, wasn't he the prom king?"

Forget ice. I'm fire now, and it's crackling in my blood. "What are you talking about?"

"Oh, no," Derek cuts in. "He wasn't just prom king. Perri told me he was the quarterback too. And you know he went on to law school."

Gabe snaps his fingers. "And wasn't it some fancy-ass law school? Yale, Harvard, something like that."

Derek nods. "Exactly. One of those Ivy League schools, and now he's a practicing attorney in San Francisco. Plus, he does all sorts of pro bono work to help lower-income families."

I remove my bow tie, so hard I might have ripped it off. "Why are you telling me this?"

"Just wanted to remind you who he was," Derek says, ever so casually.

Mr. Grayson adds, "The ladies who come in here to pick up suits for their men? They know Jamie. They talk about Jamie. From what I hear, he's quite the catch. Yessiree."

My eyes bulge. What the hell is going on? "Are you guys putting me on?"

Derek rests his hip against the counter. "Why the hell would we do that? Jamie's coming to the wedding. My sister knows him. And Jamie's stepmom is setting Vanessa up with him. Vanessa's game for it, apparently. I guess she's ready for a man who's interested in stepping off the merry-go-round, if you know what I mean."

Gabe nods to Derek. "Hey, should we invite Jamie to join our poker game? I hear he's a wiz at cards."

"He is *not* joining our poker game," I spit out, and all three men crack up.

"Look who's jelly now." Gabe laughs.

"I'm not jealous," I mutter.

I'm pissed.

I don't want this law school dude coming to the poker game. I don't want the former prom king hanging with my buds. And most of all, I definitely don't want him taking Vanessa to the wedding, or out after it, or anywhere. "Why is Jamie's stepmom setting them up?"

"Arden is all over it. So is Perri. Evidently, everyone thought it was a great idea," Gabe offers.

After he tucks his measuring tape away, Mr. Grayson raises his hand. "Just my two cents, but I think it's a brilliant idea."

I seethe. It's possible I might become a dragon. I do believe I'm breathing fire. "I don't think he should be at the wedding, and he definitely shouldn't be at the wedding with Vanessa."

Derek claps my back. "I don't know, Shaw. I think

you might need to change your stance on Jamie Sullivan. Everyone seems to think they'd make a great couple, and he's a pretty good guy. You might be seeing him more around town. Does that bother you for some reason?"

I try my damnedest to collect myself. "Why would it bother me?" I hiss in my best *I'm laid-back and cool with it* tone.

Gabe chuckles. "Man, you are going to have to come face-to-face with reality pretty damn soon."

"What reality is that?"

"Your feelings for Vanessa Marquez."

5

SHAW

The idea that she's going to the wedding with Jamie Sullivan gnaws at me the rest of the day and into the next one as I drive north toward Lake Tahoe. I'm off for the weekend, and I have a meeting there with my financial planner and my dad.

As the highway unfolds, I try to approach my frustration the way I would any other problem, by first assessing the situation.

But it's not the situation so much that irks me. It's the possible outcome.

If Vanessa is planning to go out with a guy like Jamie, that means she might wind up with a guy like him.

Or, more specifically, with *him*.

And that possibility bothers me more than I've ever been bothered by any guy she's dated.

Because Jamie is exactly the kind of guy she deserves. A good guy, a nice guy, a smart guy—a guy who would treat her really fucking well.

I hate how that winds me up.

But I don't know how to stop it.

Or what to do.

Or how I honestly feel about all of it.

When I arrive in town, I meet my dad outside the offices of my money guru. Even though Dad and I both live in Lucky Falls, I convinced him to work with my guy out of town. I wanted my dad to have enough to enjoy his retirement, more than a pension from the district attorney's office would allow, so I hooked him up with Harvey, and Dad's been making more coin to enjoy in his golden years.

But as we review portfolios, I'm distracted, and I have been since the tux shop yesterday. I can't fathom the thought of Vanessa being with Jamie. She's certainly been with other guys. She's dated other guys. Hell, I've known some of her boyfriends on and off over the years. But this one—it's like an ulcer for some damn reason.

"Your investments are quite healthy. I'd say you've fulfilled your goal of being a fireman and having quite a decent set of assets working for you," Harvey says. That was my dream—to do what I loved for a living and have the financial freedom to do it for my whole life. The pay isn't great in the fire service, but

I'm committed to the work, so by investing early and wisely, I found a way to do this job and have plenty of security.

"You've done a great job, and you're both in good positions," Harvey adds, but I can't really focus on how my portfolio is performing when all I can think about is how this other guy might perform for Vanessa.

When we leave, a slap of cold wind biting my cheeks, we agree to grab a late lunch at a nearby restaurant. Once inside, we order burgers and chat about which funds Dad wants to invest in next.

Halfway into a big bite, Dad sets his burger down and stares sharply at me. "Where are you today?"

"What do you mean?"

"You're off in la-la land, son. Where is the Shaw who loves to discuss numbers and stock tips? Where's the guy who loves to help me plan new funds to buy and sell? You okay?"

I heave a sigh. If I can't talk about this situation with my dad, who can I discuss it with? "I have a quandary."

He folds his hands. "I like quandaries. I spent my career solving them."

I put down my sandwich and wipe my hands on my napkin. "It's about Vanessa."

Dad smiles—that knowing grin of someone

who's been around the block. "I've always had a feeling a conversation with you would start this way one day."

"It's that obvious?"

"It's been clear for some time you've had it bad for her."

"That's the thing." I scratch my head. "Is it a crush? Is it lust? Is it just wanting what I can't have?"

"Those are all good questions."

"But then there's Perri. She's operating at a she-wolf level of protectiveness when it comes to Vanessa. She thinks because I've dated here and there I'm not right for her friend."

My dad snickers.

I tilt my head. "What are you laughing at?"

With crinkled eyes, he shoots me a knowing stare. "Here and there? Are you softening things for the jury?"

"Are you saying I'm a man ho, Dad?"

He holds up his hands in surrender. "I'd never use that word. But I am saying you milked every possible advantage out of the Keating family charm. Your position in the firemen's calendar too. You've never wanted for female companionship."

I straighten my shoulders. "I like the ladies, and they like me. Nothing wrong with that."

"Nothing at all. But that's part of the issue for

your sister. You've never been terribly serious with anyone, so Perri thinks you're wrong for her friend. To top it off, you don't seem sure whether you're committed about Vanessa. Seems you have a few issues to deal with."

I scrub a hand across my jaw, glad he broke it down but still perplexed as to what to do. "Guess I do have my work cut out for me."

"Which one are you going to tackle first?"

"You tell me."

He takes a drink of water, a thoughtful look in his eyes. "The most important part is how you feel for Vanessa."

That's the big one. I answer as truthfully as I can. "All I know is I don't want anyone else near her."

"You need to get to the bottom of that and understand precisely why. Once you know, then you can lay out the next steps: Are you asking Perri for permission to date Vanessa? Are you asking for permission to tell Vanessa you're in love with her? Are you wanting something else? But more than that, it comes down to this—what about Vanessa? You don't even know if she likes you. You need to figure that out, because if she doesn't feel the same, nothing else matters."

He's right. That's what I need to uncover sooner rather than later.

Sooner as in during these last days before the wedding.

After I say goodbye to my dad and slide into my truck, my phone rings.

What do you know? It's *sooner* calling.

6

SHAW

With the phone cradled between my neck and shoulder, I rub my hands together, trying to warm up as I turn on the truck's heater. Tahoe is balls-cold this time of year. "You're saying your grandpa was going to help you get the cabin ready?"

"Yes. He was going to do all that, you know, *manly* stuff," she says with a laugh, since we both know she doesn't like handling those tasks. "Check the fireplace. Test the stove. Do stuff to the water heater. Make sure the gutters are un-guttered. You know what I mean."

I laugh lightly. "All the things you don't want to do."

"Exactly. I freely admit I detest things with knobs and wires that require tools and hammers." She emits a shuddering sound that's horror-flick cringe-worthy. I start to make a knob joke—because she can't really detest a knob that can hammer well—but since I'm now officially jockeying for pole position with Jamie "Mr. Perfect" Sullivan, I might need to dial down the usual banter.

Be a little more sophisticated.

"Tools can be confounding," I say.

"Exactly. Now, if Perri was around, I'd have her do that stuff. But since I'm getting the cabin ready for her honeymoon as a wedding gift, it was going to be Gramps and me. He was going to do all the maintenance, and I was going to change the bedding and set out towels, and make sure they had plenty of pretty shampoo and body wash."

"I'm sure Derek will love the body wash. Make sure to get him a gardenia or lavender-scented one." I'm not turning off the humor hose completely.

"Very funny. The body wash is for Perri."

"Like I said, I'm sure Derek will enjoy the body wash," I say, then it's my turn to cringe, horror movie–style. "Wait. Let's not talk about my sister and body wash. Back to Gramps. What happened? Is he busy at the horse ranch?"

Shortly after her granddad moved his family to the States two decades ago, he began working as a ranch manager and eventually went on to buy his own spread. Now he owns one in Nevada as well as the cabin here in Tahoe. He did well for himself for sure.

"Nope. He's just not feeling so great. He has a stomach bug, and he's staying at their main home an hour away."

I pride myself on my iron stomach, glad it's made of metal. "That's no fun."

"I know. He was planning on coming over this afternoon, but he has a date with the porcelain god. So Arden and I were on the phone, trying to figure out if I could find a local handyman. It's getting late though."

"I'll do it." There's no way I'll let another man save the day for her.

"Well, that was easy. Arden said that Gabe mentioned you were up here meeting with your finance guy, so I was hoping you were still around. I don't have a clue how those dang fireplaces work. You're handy, right?"

I puff out my chest. "Damn straight. No fireman worth his salt is un-handy."

"And you're worth your salt, I presume," she says, a little flirty. "And you're not too far away." Her tone is the most inviting I've ever heard.

I smile, loving the direction this is heading. "I'm pretty damn close. Give me the address."

She does, and I tell her I'll be there in forty minutes.

Yup. There's no time like the present to figure out my feelings, to sort lust from jealousy or from something more.

I drive straight toward the cabin, following Google Map's route as the robotic lady's voice tells me to take this winding turn up this hilly road then that steeper curve up an even steeper street. The whole time, the sky turns a hazy shade of orange around the edges, the clouds billowing, swelling with a hint of snow.

By the time I pull into the driveway, up here in Steepville on the corner of Steepington Avenue and Holy Shit That's Steep Road, the ground is coated in the first flurries.

I hope they fall fast and furious.

We get foul weather in Lucky Falls now and again, but nothing that necessitates snow boots. Today, I say thank you to Old Man Winter when Vanessa greets me on the porch decked out in peel-me-off jeans, fluffy boots, a white knit cap, and a red-striped sweater that fits in an eye-popping kind of way. I know fuck all about fashion, but since Vanessa wears retro stuff pretty much all the time, I'm guessing that's some fifties-style sweater.

And if the fifties were all about breast-hugging tops, God bless that decade. That sweater is doing things to her tits that might drive me insane with lust.

But I'm nearly already there.

"Hey, snow bunny."

"Hey, snowman," she says, wrapping her arms around her waist, and her remark throws me. Snow bunnies are sexy; snowmen are definitely not. Has she just friend-zoned me in favor of Jamie?

Oh, hell no.

That is one zone I won't go into without a fight.

I point to the house. "Get inside, woman." A flicker of something—perhaps interest—flickers across her warm brown eyes. "I don't want you to freeze."

"I know, but I wanted to say hi and thank you. Also, hurry on in. It's snowing. And yes, I know I just pointed out the obvious." Then she adds with a sexy little pout, "But that's because I'm a helpful snow bunny."

Laughing, and liking that she's using her nickname, I look up at the sky as it tosses flakes at us like confetti. "It is indeed snowing. As much as I'd like to trade more snow names with you, let me tend to the gutters first since, well, I don't imagine you want to have it on your conscience if I have to climb up on the roof later in a blinding snowstorm, during which I trip, tumble to the ground, and am left to the coyotes as night falls."

"But I bet you'd be a tasty icicle for coyotes," she says, and I'll hang my hat on that one adjective—*tasty*—as I claw my way out of snowman zone.

"I make a very good popsicle."

Her eyes dance with mischief, and I'm ready to pump a fist. From snowman to something you suck on in twenty seconds flat. Go me.

"I'll open the garage. Everything you'll need is in there. Gramps said he had a chimney sweep come out at the end of the summer, so I don't think you need to worry about the full works. But can you check and make sure there's not a dead raccoon in there?"

I give a tip of the cap. "Raccoon inspection, at your service."

"And while you're inspecting the chimney, I'll stock up on the items that shall not be named for Perri and Derek." She drops her voice to an alluring whisper. "*Seductive body wash. Tropical island-scented lotion. Sexy candles.*"

I shudder, slamming my hands over my ears. Vanessa laughs, her smile wide and bright.

When I let go of my ears, she points to the house. "And after I do all the womanly stuff, how about I whip up a delicious hot chocolate? I picked up supplies at the market, and you're definitely going to need warming up."

I'd like to warm her *up, all night long.*

"Count me in."

7

SHAW

An hour and a half later, I'm finished with the roof detail, and the sun is dropping in the sky.

Carefully, I climb down the ladder, set the tools neatly in the garage, and return to the porch. Beneath the fine dusting of flakes are pine needles and dried leaves, so I grab the broom I spotted in the garage and sweep those up, then I do the steps too.

Nothing wrong with going above and beyond.

Satisfied with my labors so far and hopeful about their ability to impress a woman—since that's key in any manual labor—I stomp the snow off my work boots and rap on the door.

A few seconds later, Vanessa opens it, the hinges squealing in misery. "One, you don't have to knock. Two, I think the door needs a little oil."

I smile mischievously, unable to resist the low-hanging fruit. "Nothing wrong with a little lube now and then."

She snickers, shaking her head in amusement.

Guess I can't quite dial down the banter all the way. But who wants an off-switch on a dirty mind anyway?

I find the WD-40, oil up the hinges, and return the can to the garage once more. Then I tug open the newly silent door, dusting snowflakes off my hair.

Vanessa scurries over. "Wait. You still have some snowflakes on you." Reaching up, she lightly swipes a hand over my head.

Why, thank you, manual labor. Thank you very much.

"I think you missed a spot." I tap the back of my skull.

With a smile, she brushes her hand against me once more. I nearly purr. I might even arch my back.

I head inside, shed my coat, remove my boots, and issue a report. "The gutters are cleaned, the chimney is topped off with a quick brushing, and as a special bonus just for you, there are no raccoon bodies inside it."

She breathes a big sigh of relief. "Oh, thank God. Not just for us, but for the wildlife."

"It's best for everyone if the raccoons get to keep being bandits." I lift my nose, catching a whiff of something. "What did you do in here? It smells like . .

." As I step into the spacious living room, I sniff a little more, trying to detect the scent. "Like juniper and sage maybe? Hey, are you secretly a Starbucks barista whipping up juniper lattes?"

She shuts the door behind me, reaching for my coat and hanging it on a hook by the door. "As a matter of fact, in the last hour, I've converted this cabin into a clandestine Starbucks. Be prepared for an onslaught of lumberjacks and wood nymphs."

"You don't say?"

"Word is there are plenty of both around here."

"I was aware of lumberjacks, but wood nymphs who like coffee drinks? That's news to me."

"Have you had those juniper lattes? They're incredible."

"You won't get any argument from me."

She arches a brow. "You don't seem like the kind of guy who orders a juniper latte. How did you wind up with one?" Then her face darkens, and she shakes her head. "That was a stupid question. You probably had one on a date."

She spins around, heading for the kitchen, and I need to dispel that notion right now, even though I am savoring the hint of jealousy in the word *date*. "I didn't have one on a date. Mrs. Jansen bought me one when I helped her fix a broken pipe in her yarn shop."

With a glance back at me, Vanessa's eyes brighten

again, like that was the best answer in the world. "You helped fix a pipe for her?"

I nod. "Sure did. Got a pipe you need me to fix?" There's a dirty connotation in there somewhere, but I'm not sure it needs to be jumped on.

"I don't think so. But you never know. Also, I used some juniper-and-sage room spray after I cleaned. I swept up and vacuumed while you were on the roof."

Granted, I didn't get a great look at the place before, but it looks pretty damn good now. "You're speedy. And the cabin both looks and smells good. I'm sure the newlyweds will appreciate it."

"I hope so. And I know I owe you that hot chocolate. But I ran into a tiny problem when I was starting to make it." She wiggles her fingers so I will follow her to the kitchen.

She taps the edge of the stove. "Burner won't turn on."

"Dr. Handyman at your service." I mime donning a stethoscope then check out the stove, giving it an inspection and listening to its heartbeat. She chuckles as I go. I pretend to snap off rubber gloves as I issue my pronouncement. "And the diagnosis is . . . you have a faulty igniter."

Her eyes widen in mock outrage. "Take that back. I do not have a faulty igniter."

And she's being flirty right back.

I make a note of that in the back of my libido. I mean, my brain. I tuck it away in my brain.

But then a voice reminds me this isn't a new style of interaction. Vanessa has always played on the teasing side of the fence.

I step a little closer, my eyes locking on hers as I take my time, my voice going low, raspy. "I don't know anything about your igniter, but I highly doubt it's faulty."

"It's definitely not faulty," she whispers, a hint of desire floating on her words.

"I'll just make sure." For a few seconds, the air seems to hum and crackle. Like we're not going to fix stoves or check fireplaces. Like we're going to rip off clothes. Then I'll hoist her on the counter and wrap those legs around my hips. Kiss the breath out of her. Drive her wild with my lips and hands and body.

Instead, I focus on helping her, since that seems to get this woman going. I fix the stove while she tells me what she worked on inside the cabin. She turned on the hot tub to make sure it heats up properly (Gramps cleaned it a few weeks ago), changed all the bedding, straightened all the rooms, hung fresh towels, and scrubbed the bathrooms. "I even checked to make sure the water runs and isn't rusty. See? I have a handy side."

I shake a finger at her, chiding. "Don't be taking my job away."

"I would never do that. Just trying to be helpful."

"You're very helpful. And you've made this cabin quite lovely."

"Hey, are you hungry? I picked up sandwiches at the market."

I pat my stomach, shaking my head. "Nope. Had a late lunch with my dad. But thanks for offering. Maybe later." And I leave it at that, because later would be good.

"Yes, later," she says, agreeing, and I like her answer very much.

As I finish the stove, she tilts her head as if she's deep in thought. "Should we chop wood for the fireplace? There's a bit on the deck, but it won't last long."

I lean my head back and laugh.

"What's so funny? Don't you know how to chop firewood?"

"Course I do. I'm a fireman. I can handle an ax just fine. I just thought it was funny when you said *we*. Don't worry—I'm not letting *you* handle an ax."

One eyebrow rises. "You think I can't handle an ax?"

"I think it's dangerous for anyone who doesn't know how to use one. Plus, I'd love to make sure you have enough firewood to be warm and toasty. So I'll go outside and play Paul Bunyan for you," I say with a wink.

"Then I'll make sure I have hot chocolate for you when you come back in." She flicks a lock of chestnut hair off her shoulder. "Think you'd like a little treat?"

Does she even know how sexy she sounds when she asks that question?

"I do want a treat," I tell her, but the treat is already here—us alone in this cabin as afternoon spills into evening.

That's the best treat I could have.

As she grabs milk, a bag of gourmet chocolates, and some spices, I head outside to chop some wood. As I work, the snow falls softly and quietly, with no sign of stopping as nighttime tiptoes into Tahoe. Doesn't take a genius to realize we aren't leaving this cabin anytime soon, or likely even tonight.

I stack the wood, return the ax, and head back inside, where I find Vanessa whipping up what smells like a delicious drink.

I whistle in appreciation as she wields whisks, spoons, and chocolate with deftness. "Damn, woman, you are a gourmand."

"I'm of the belief that there are two kinds of people in the world: those who like chocolate made with water"—her gagging face says exactly what she thinks about that—"and those who like it made with milk." She smiles devilishly.

"And what kind do you think I am?"

As she stirs the pot, she studies my face. "I think you're the kind who's going to enjoy what I give you."

A groan rumbles up my chest. "That is exactly the kind of man I am."

A few minutes later, my mouth is watering as she pours the chocolate mixture into two mugs. I reach for mine, but she swats my hand away. "What the hell? You're toying with me. It's sitting here, tempting me, and you won't let me have it?"

"It needs to cool off, Shaw. And while it does, I'm going to tease you even more," she says, and yanks open the fridge. She comes back brandishing a canister of whipped cream.

I like her style of teasing. "When did you become such a taunter?"

"When we got snowed in," she tosses back as she dispenses some whipped cream on top of the steaming mug of chocolate then on my nose.

Yup. She's dropped a delicious and provocative substance on my body.

Maybe not the first body part I had in mind for whipped-cream kink, but I'll take what I can get. I move a little closer to her. "And now how do you propose I get that off my nose, snow bunny?"

Her smile is magnetic. It's sweet and dirty at the same time. "I don't know, snow devil. How do you want to get it off?"

Dear Lord. Did she take extra foxy pills today? I

reach for her hand and slide my fingers along her palm, noting the hitch in her breath. Correction: noting it and loving it.

I drag her finger along the whipped cream on my nose, watching her eyes go bigger, wider. And because there's no time like the present, I bring her finger to my mouth.

And lick off the whipped cream.

She gasps.

"My turn," I murmur. Grabbing the whipped cream, I drop a dot on her cute nose.

She stares at me inquisitively. "And am I licking it off now? Or are you?" Her tone is purely coy, thoroughly playful.

This time, I swipe off the cream, and before either of us can say a word, she grabs my finger and licks it off me, humming around the tip.

Holy fuck.

Vanessa swirls her tongue, licking and, dare I say, *simulating*, and also *stimulating*, as she gives me one snug, tight suck and a flick of her tongue, as if she's letting me know what she'd like to do.

I'm starting to get some answers to my questions.

More than *starting*.

I want more of this woman. Pretty sure I want all of her. The question remains, what does she want from me?

8

VANESSA

Well, that escalated quickly.

It's not as if I asked Shaw to the cabin to seduce him with whipped cream, and I definitely didn't buy it for that purpose. I'm not even into food play.

And yet I completely wanted his finger in my mouth. When I get near him, I want him madly.

Most of the time, there's a built-in barrier between us. A sex blockade in the presence of other people. I haven't been alone with him in ages, and that's made it easy, relatively speaking, to ignore the ache inside me.

Now that it's only the two of us, my want is like a parrot on my shoulder, squawking, demanding crackers. Yes, Polly, I want a Shaw cracker too.

I grab my mug like it's a shield so I can sort out my

thoughts. "It's snowing harder." Grasping that excuse to snag a little space, I head to the living room, set the mug on the coffee table, and march to the window. Outside, the snow falls faster, heavier. I point to the white carpet blanketing the ground. "Look! I think we're here for a little while." The thought of being stuck with him tonight is both nerve-wracking and thrilling.

Will it last all night?

I grab my phone from the coffee table to check the weather app.

"What's the report?" he asks as he walks over from the kitchen.

I shrug. "No service, but I'm not surprised. It tends to be pretty spotty at the best of times. I managed to get a signal at the end of the driveway when I called you earlier."

After putting his cup on the table too, he joins me at the window, his shoulder nearly touching mine. "Then the Shaw Keating Amateur Meteorologist Report says . . . it sure looks like it's going to snow all night."

But does he *want* it this way? Does his parrot want a cracker too? Does he even have a parrot for me?

I try to keep the mood light, easy, and bird-free. "That's Tahoe for you. One minute it's sunshine and smiles, the next it's snowstorms."

He stares through the glass at the sky. "Bet it's going to last the whole day."

My eyes stray to the clock above the mantel. It's nearly eight. "The whole night is more like it."

He turns his face, his gaze catching mine. His eyes darken, his voice deepens. "Looks like we'll have to figure out how to pass the time."

My throat goes dry. Is he saying what I think he's saying? Or is he flirting like the gold medalist flirt he's been my whole life? "We have board games," I blurt out. "That's what you do in a cabin to pass the time, right?"

A grin seems to tug at his lips. "Absolutely. Break out Monopoly. Bring on Chutes and Ladders. Let's go crazy with Candy Land."

I tilt my head, giving him a sharp stare. "Do you think I don't know you're teasing?"

He holds up his hands in surrender. "I love Candy Land. I swear. Let's play it after we finish the most amazing hot chocolate ever."

"Fine. Hot chocolate and Candy Land it is."

I wish it were hot chocolate and kisses . . . kisses and stripping . . . stripping and hot, sweaty fireplace sex . . . hot, sweaty fireplace sex and promises.

But Candy Land it'll be for now.

We move to the couch. He's quiet at first as he reaches for his mug. "It's a damn good thing we have hot chocolate as well. To pass the time."

"Try it first. But if you don't like my special hot chocolate, we can never be friends again," I say, feeling the need to emphasize our friendship, perhaps so I can figure out if that's where he still is. Just because I sucked on his finger like it was his dick doesn't mean anything more will come of it. After all, we're whiling away the hours drinking cocoa, not licking whipped cream from each other's navels.

But when I say "friends," he looks like he's chewing on the word and it tastes like kale to him.

When I chew on the word, it tastes a little like guilt.

Like dark secrets I should bury forever.

I'm here in this cabin for Perri, as a wedding gift to my amazing friend. I didn't drive up from Lucky Falls to seduce her brother. Her handsome, funny, sexy brother who I've been longing for over the years.

He taps the side of the mug. "Since we're friends, why don't you tell me what makes this hot chocolate so special?"

"Cinnamon."

"Ah, so it has a little spice," he says, his hazel eyes dancing playfully.

Briefly, I wonder if Jamie's eyes will lure me the same way. Whether any other man can possibly have this effect on me. No one has before, and perhaps that's why I haven't found *the one*. Maybe that's the reason I want the real deal but haven't had it yet. Have I compared all my boyfriends to him? To a man I've never had?

All I want is to learn if the comparison is valid. And to do so by tasting the chocolate on his lips.

"Yes, it gives it a little kick," I answer, fighting to focus on the hot chocolate. Fighting like my sanity depends on it.

"I like a little kick," he says, and he makes it so hard not to flirt, especially as his eyes drift to my sweater, and to what's underneath the material.

I happen to have nice boobs. They're round, firm C-cups, which is kind of awesome. I like my breasts. I like my body, for all its curves, dips, and blips.

He lifts his chin. "By the way, what's up with the striped sweater?"

I pluck at the knitting. "You don't like my sweater?"

"No, I think it's fantastic. I mean, is it part of your whole retro-girl look?"

"It is. I snagged it from a vintage shop on Etsy. I think I'm incapable of wearing clothes that were made in this century."

"I've always noticed that you sort of look like you just stepped out of the 1950s, which, trust me, is great. But I'm curious why."

I love that he's asking. We've talked about so much over the years, at parties, at dinners, at the bowling alley. But here's a new thing that we're chatting about. "When we moved to the United States, one of the ways I practiced English was watching TV and movies. I loved *Happy Days* and Elvis Presley flicks—that whole vintage look. It felt very American to me. By the time I started making choices about what I wanted to wear, that was the time period I identified with."

"That is one of the coolest stories I've ever heard."

"It is?" A dose of delight zips through me. "Why?"

"Because it's a reason. It's not just 'Oh, I think it's cute.' Not that there's anything wrong with that. But you had a deeper reason. It says something about who you are."

"I suppose it did. Maybe it still does."

"Is that something you wanted when you first came here? To feel more American? I knew you then, but we were, what, six and seven? I don't remember a ton."

"We were young," I say, recalling only bits and pieces of when my parents moved to California from Colombia so my scientist father could pursue better job opportunities. "I already knew enough English, but I wanted to fit in. I can seamlessly fit in now, and clearly I can speak without an accent. But here's a little-known fact—I still dream in Spanish."

He inches closer. It's heady, his nearness. It

makes the air crackle, and I'm thoroughly distracted once more. Especially when he asks in that low, smoky voice, "What else do you do in Spanish?"

My breath hitches, and my stomach flips. I try to think of Perri and how I've been lying to her for years by omission . . . but I'm also not thinking about Perri at all. I can't keep her in my head when Shaw looks at me like he wants to be more than friends.

Like he wants to pass the time the same damn way I do. I decide to tango closer to the truth because I need to know if it's time to break out Monopoly so I don't jump him—or if it's time to jump him. "Sometimes, when I'm really caught up in something, I'll speak in Spanish."

A naughty grin spreads on his face. "Is that so?"

"Yes."

He seems to know what I mean and where I'm heading. He's staring at me with fire in his eyes. With hunger in his expression. My whole body sizzles, and I want to back up and revise my answer about how I want to pass the time.

I want to tell him the truth now because my life is barreling toward a date with another man. A man who might very well be the real thing. But I don't want to go anywhere with anyone else until I know what to do with this massive, overstuffed box of feelings for my best friend's brother.

Maybe it's time to open the box and get this man

out of my system. Perhaps that's why I haven't found *the one* yet—because I'm hung up on *this one* I can't have. And maybe, if I have him once, if we "pass the time," I won't think of him anymore. I'll empty the box, fold it up, stuff it in the recycling bin, and walk away.

He nudges my knee with his. "Vanessa," he says playfully. "What exactly do you mean when you say 'caught up'?"

This is it. This is the chance the snowfall is giving me—to tell Shaw I need him to rid me of my desire for him. He's the sickness and he's the cure.

But how do I say *I speak in Spanish when I'm thinking of you? I say your name in my native tongue when I slide my hand down my body at night. When you make me come in my fantasies. When I call out your name.*

I take a deep breath.

You say it by saying it.

So I do, needing to crack open the box.

I say all of that in a rush of lightning-fast Spanish.

He blinks. "What?"

But I backpedal, because I want him to go first. I want him to want me so badly he dreams of me in Spanish, and he doesn't even speak the language. "I said, when something tastes good, I say it in Spanish."

He shakes his head as if he's caught me. He leans closer, his eyes holding my gaze. "I don't think that's what you were saying."

My stomach flips. A rush of heat zips through me. "What do you think I was saying?"

His eyes blaze. "I think you were saying something else."

I glance at the fireplace, trying to find the courage but wanting him to find it too. I wrap my arms around my waist.

"Do you want me to build a fire?"

Sex and a fireplace? "Yes."

He heads to the deck, grabs a few logs, and builds a fire. When it's lit, he turns around and offers me his hand.

I gaze at his big hand. This is a clear step, and that's what I've wanted from him.

I take it, loving the feel of his fingers wrapped around mine.

He pulls me up from the couch. "Want to sit by the fire?"

I'm *on* fire. "Yes."

He tugs me down to the carpet in front of the flames. We sit cross-legged, looking at each other. "We're not drinking hot cocoa to pass the time," I whisper.

He shakes his head. "We're not playing board games to pass the time."

Right here looking at me is the man I've been in love with for more than a decade. He's the one I want to go to the wedding with. He's the one I either need to get under or get over.

"I'm supposed to go to Perri's wedding with Jamie Sullivan," I say, ripping off part of the Band-Aid.

His jaw ticks. His eyes narrow. "I heard," he mutters as he lets go of my hand.

My brow knits. "You heard? What, is it like a rumor going around?"

"Doesn't sound like it's a rumor. Sounds like the truth." And he sounds annoyed. "Is it true?" His voice is harsher than I've ever heard it, but I like what that knife's edge in it tells me.

"Perri and Arden want me to go with him. It was Miriam's idea."

He's silent for a beat, then he studies me like he can find all my truths in my eyes. "Is that what you want?"

Now.

This moment.

It's time.

I straighten my shoulders, returning to another question from before. "What do you think I said in Spanish?"

He stares at me, undressing me with his eyes, licking his lips. Then he rises on his knees, and the world slows.

It slides into this moment where he lifts his hand. Cups my cheek. Runs the pad of his thumb across my face.

I burn with longing.

And I melt from the terrifyingly wonderful awareness that this is happening.

He inches closer, his mouth on a fast track for mine, and whispers, "I think you said *this*."

He captures my lips in a kiss.

9
SHAW

I have a favorite kiss.

It wasn't a hot and heavy one. It wasn't one that led to frenzied, fevered sex.

The one that tops my list was nearly innocent. A mere brush of lips as "Have Yourself A Merry Little Christmas" played at my parents' house one weekend when I was home from college.

Ten years ago, my friends gathered during break, drinking spiked eggnog, eating gingerbread cookies, and knocking back beer and wine.

I'd headed down the hallway to grab a bottle of wine, passing under the mistletoe that my parents—away in Mexico—had hung above a doorway.

When I turned around, Vanessa was walking toward me, wearing a red-and-white-checkered dress and a Mrs. Claus hat, looking like the hottest Santa's helper I'd ever seen.

She'd had a few glasses of champagne. I'd had a few beers.

Was it the liquor? The music? The way the lights from the tree twinkled in her brown eyes?

Her gaze drifted upward to the sprig of mistletoe, and she stopped under it, wearing an inviting little grin. I walked to her, accepting her invitation on the spot. "Merry Christmas, Vanessa," I'd said, then swept my lips over hers.

She'd gasped, a sweet and delicious sound that wove through my entire body. On her lips I tasted gingerbread and champagne, and a little lip gloss too. I'd been buzzed from the drinks, but then it was from the possibilities, from the idea that I could wrap a hand around her waist, jerk her close, and kiss the breath out of her. I could take her upstairs and have her, like I'd always wanted to.

I pressed one more kiss to those fantastic lips. Before I spiraled into a haze of Nat King Cole and her, I forced myself to stop.

I had to get away, or I'd want more than one kiss.

"Merry Christmas," I'd said, and walked off, the memory of one sweet kiss lingering with me for weeks.

Hell, for years.

But this?

Here in front of the fire? With my hand cupping her jaw, her lithe body warm, and her lips parted?

I'm not walking away. I'm seeing this through.

This is my new favorite kiss, and nothing will top it. I brush my lips over hers, and the taste of her—chocolate and sweetness and that hint of gloss—lights me up.

As our mouths collide, my thoughts go foggy. My body sparks. Electricity shoots through every damn vein, cell, and molecule.

This is the only way to kiss.

No one to find us, not a soul to stumble down the hall. And no one to remind us why we shouldn't do this.

No one except us, and I'm not issuing that reminder tonight.

Because . . . we *should* do this.

I hold her tighter and deepen the kiss. My tongue skates over hers, and our lips devour each other.

I heat up everywhere, and it's not from the flames in the fireplace. It's from how she responds. From the way she loops her hands around my neck, tugging me closer. She kisses me with a ferocity I've dreamed of, with a passion that underscores years.

Like she's wanted to kiss me for ages.

My God, that's what I've wanted—to know how she feels under my touch. Our lips explore each other's desperately, like we're running out of time, running out of air. But we don't care. We need *this*.

The temperature in me ratchets to the sky as I claim her mouth with mine. Her hands thread into the back of my hair. Like a desperate woman, she jerks me closer.

I'm a desperate man, and I want us to be as close as possible. But this position isn't going to work much longer, me on my knees, her slinking under me—it's good, but I'm about to topple over, so I slide her down to the floor.

She moans, opening her legs for me. I groan, a carnal growl. I don't think I can stop groaning, because . . . holy fuck. Vanessa Marquez is arching her back and rocking her hips into me in front of the fireplace, and I'm in my perfect dirty heaven, even though we have clothes on.

Stupid clothes.

But hell if I'm breaking this connection. This mind-blowing, skin-sizzling connection as our bodies grind faster. Her fingers twist in my hair, tugging and pulling, and her noises—they grow louder, more insistent. Like desperate pleas.

I kiss harder. I can't stop kissing her, can't stop wanting her.

I rub against her, and my hard-as-stone dick announces all its plans. *Get inside her. Feel her warm heat wrapping around my length.*

With that image in mind, I press my hard-on *right there*, where she wants me. Instantly, she moans, swiveling her hips. Push, grind, press, groan. We're dry-fucking.

Which is awesome, but also not the endgame.

I need real fucking, and this woman needs it too.

I pull back and look at her face, her hazy, sex-drunk eyes. Finally, at last, I say the words that have spun on my tongue for years. "I want you so fucking much, Vanessa. I want you now. I want to make you feel so good. That's how I want to pass the time with you."

Her lips part in a sensual *yes*, then she says something in Spanish, practically purring the foreign words.

I laugh. "You're going to need to translate."

She yanks me closer, gazes into my eyes, and whispers, "I said, 'I've never wanted anyone like this.'"

Did I say nothing would top that kiss?

I was wrong. Because everything keeps getting better and better.

Like right now.

I kneel and tug off my sweater to find she's the fastest undresser in the West. The second my T-shirt's off, she's tossed her sweater on the couch, and is unhooking her bra.

My brain short-circuits, but even as the wires fry, I retain some semblance of rational thought. And I need a moment.

I really fucking do.

Because . . . her bra.

It's black lace with a pink bow between the cups, and it's the most enticing piece of lingerie ever worn.

Then it's . . . not worn. She throws it to the couch, and I'm like a pinball machine lighting up. The buzzers whir, the flippers flap, and I hit the high score.

Vanessa's. Tits. Are. Exposed.

The beautiful vixen that she is—she knows they're fantastic. She knows I'm in heaven. She smiles coyly at me, giving me a *come and get 'em* look.

"Thought you might enjoy," she whispers, and my dick leaps up, like he could high-five me. He knows he's getting what he wants tonight.

My hands dart out to cup the beauties.

Soft, alluring, perfect teardrops.

I must have been very good in a past life to get to hold this lushness.

It's possible I am whimpering. But who could blame me? These tits are my kryptonite, and they can take me down anytime.

"Why, oh why, did you wait so long to take off

your shirt for me?" I bury my face between the two gorgeous globes and worship them.

She laughs, and she moans at the same time.

Then she stops laughing as I kiss her soft flesh, drawing one rosy nipple into my mouth. She tastes heavenly. I savor every lick as I lavish all the attention I can on these lovelies, until she's panting so fast she might actually come this way. Which would be fine by me.

But she pushes me away from her chest, holding my face hard in her hands. She stares at me with a wild intensity. "That's why. Because I knew you're a junkie. Now, have you had your fix?"

I quirk up my lips. "You think that's all I need of these perfect tits, snow bunny?"

She smiles devilishly. "I think that's all you're getting right now. I want you someplace else." Rocking her hips up against me, she lets me know exactly where that is.

I fucking love that she's direct. That she's no shrinking violet. She's telling me what she needs, and I intend to satisfy every last requirement.

I slide a hand between her legs, cupping her through the denim. She's so fucking warm. "Mmm. I have a feeling this is where you want me."

Her eyes float closed, and she lets herself fall back on her elbows on the rug, arching up into my touch. My God, she's so stunning like that, sensual and sexy, shirtless and asking me to please her.

It would be my pleasure indeed.

"Stay there," I tell her.

"I'm not going anywhere."

I stand, grab a pillow from the couch, and bring it back to her, tucking it under her head. "There you go."

"Aren't you sweet?"

"Woman, I simply don't want you to hurt your head, since I'm going to be fucking you hard."

She shudders, biting her lip. "You are?"

I grab my wallet from my back pocket, flip it open, and snag a condom. "I'd like to. That work for you?"

"I told you, Shaw. I've never wanted anyone like this," she says, her voice steady and confident. That certainty is a hook, latching right on to my heart.

Gazing down at her, half naked and waiting for me, sharpens the lens on my mission to figure this out.

To figure *us* out.

Right now, I've unearthed a key detail—we want each other the same way.

I kneel next to her, hold her cheek, and meet her gaze. "Vanessa." My voice is stripped bare. "I've never, not once in my whole life, wanted anyone even one-tenth as much as I want you."

She lets out a deep exhale, as if she's relieved.

Maybe happy too.

So am I.

For a second, maybe more, I feel like I'm living in a dream. Because this is everything I've fantasized about. For years.

"It's the same for me," she murmurs, as she lifts her hips and unzips her jeans. Like a statue, I'm frozen, absorbing the moment. Vanessa undressing for me—that's one hell of an answer.

I unfreeze and go from zero to sixty in seconds, shucking off my jeans.

"Come on. Hurry. I'm dying here," she urges.

"I'm getting naked, woman. Give me a hot minute."

She sits up, pulling on the cuffs of my jeans. "Faster, faster."

I laugh as I tear them off, nearly tripping. She chuckles too, and it occurs to me that this could have been a supremely awkward moment. Or a weighty, silent one. It might also have been darkly clandestine. But it feels like us. Like two people who've known each other a long time, and who are doing the next natural thing.

I tug off my briefs, and when my dick is free, she stares hungrily, taking a deep breath. Then she murmurs something in her native tongue.

"Are you caught up in the moment?" I kneel in front of her, peeling off her black lace panties.

Then I'm the one caught up, because she's fucking beautiful. One chestnut landing strip—otherwise, she's bare. God, I want to taste her, eat her, devour her pussy. She's so damn wet and slick.

"I'm so caught up in the moment," she says, then eyes the condom. "Please."

I roll it on then settle between her legs. And that's when it hits me. Yes, we are still us, laughing, joking, teasing. But right now, we're also something new entirely.

We're lovers.

We're not just friends, two people who've been in each other's lives forever.

We're a man and a woman, naked in the dark, and we're going to be coming together. All that laughter and teasing slinks away as I place my hands on her thighs, spreading her open. "V," I say, husky and low.

"Shaw."

A groan echoes in my throat. "God, I want you so fucking much. I'm dying for you, baby. Just dying."

"Me too. That's what I was saying just now. I was saying how much I want you."

I rub the head of my cock against her, and she bows her back, murmuring *yes*. She lets her knees fall apart.

I push in, sinking deeper, making contact with all that glorious heat, until I'm all the way in. And it's electric. It's intense. It's fucking breathtaking.

I move in her, slowly at first, searching for her rhythm.

She slides her hands along my back, and I shudder. "Love that. Do that."

"Yeah?"

"Yeah."

She digs her nails in, and I pump harder, deeper. So deep she cries out, my name a long, carnal song on her tongue.

"Fuck, I love it when you say my name like that," I whisper as I swivel my hips and drive into her.

"Shaw," she murmurs. "I . . ."

I'm at a loss for words too.

Everything is sensation as I thrust.

Her wetness enveloping me.

Her soft flesh arching beneath me.

Her nails scoring my back.

Her hands gripping my ass.

Her breath coming faster.

It's almost too much. My bones crackle, pleasure barreling through me on a mad dash for my groin. But that won't do. I have one job—make her toes curl.

Gritting my teeth and fighting off the threat of my

own orgasm, I hike up her hip, wrapping her leg around me, going deeper.

"So good, bunny. So fucking good."

"Better than good." Running her hands up to my hair, she wraps her fingers around my head, looking in my eyes. And we shift yet again. From friends to lovers to something more profound.

Yes, I'm fucking her.

Yes, it's fantastic.

And yes, sex has been known to fry a man's brain.

But this feels like a helluva lot more than a way to pass the time.

The sounds she makes unravel me. They make me burn everywhere with rabid lust. They turn my thoughts hazy.

She cries out, and then she does what she promised. She's talking in Spanish, and I don't know this language. But even I understand what she's saying.

Oh God.

So good.

Yes.

Yes.

Yes!

I'm willing to bet the next one is something like this...

Coming!

Hottest sound ever. Her accent when she loses

control, when she gives herself to pleasure, turns me on so much I can feel myself unraveling. She arches, shuddering, and I chase her there, groaning and growling until I reach my release, the snow a mad blur outside the windows, the world beyond the cabin spiraling away.

After, I need to know if we're simply passing the time or if we're starting something new. I want the latter. I want to start something with her and keep it going and going.

But when she lifts a brow and offers a suggestion for what's next on the schedule, I don't know that I'm getting the answer tonight.

Or that I mind.

10

BOOK CLUB LADIES GROUP CHAT

CarolAnn: Dying here! Give us the details. Is everything firmed up for the wedding?

Miriam: Can you hear me squealing across town? It absolutely is. I can just picture them together having a dance, maybe a bite of Sara's coconut cake, toasting to the happy new couple. It's all so picture-perfect.

Sara: My heart is fluttering! (Though I'm not baking a cake for a wedding! Puh-leeze. That's only for my man.) But this outcome almost makes me want to try to set up CarolAnn's handsome paramedic nephew with my niece. You know, the one who works at Arden's bookstore. What do you say?

CarolAnn: Yes! Madeline would be perfect for Hunter. He's a teddy bear, and she's a smarty-pants.

Miriam: Being a retired teacher, that's my favorite kind of gal to set up. The paramedic and the bookstore gal are next on our list! Once this first project is complete, of course, in a few more days.

Sara: These youngsters just need a little nudge sometimes. And when they are so right for each other, they don't always see what's in front of their noses.

Miriam: Truer words. And you two may have given me a hard time about how long it took, but it never would have happened if we hadn't intervened. Am I right?

Sara: Right, yes. Smooth, no.

Miriam: Smoothness is overrated. All that matters is these two young lovers are coming together! We simply had to be involved.

CarolAnn: They do need go-getters like us to move them along. And we know how to wring the most out of our lives.

Sara: Nobody does life better than us.

11

VANESSA

I dip a toe into the bubbling water. "It's toasty," I declare as stars twinkle in the inky sky. I shiver as the chilly night air wraps around me.

But I'll be hot in seconds.

Shaw peers at the hot tub. "It damn well better be boiling since it's colder than a polar bear's pinkie outside." He glances toward the back door—I wedged a brick in it. I'm no dummy. I've heard stories of people who freeze to death in outdoor hot tubs on back decks when the door locks behind them. The keys, bathrobes, and towels are all on a chair right outside the glass door.

Which is unlocked.

We're triple-covered, though, because Shaw raps his knuckles on the window he's also cracked open.

"That way I won't have to break out the ax and bust down the door if we did get locked outside."

"But you could, right?" I untie the bathrobe and drop it on the wooden deck.

His eyes bulge.

"Could what?" He sounds transfixed.

I step into the hot tub, and I roll my hands, reminding him of the conversation. "You could break down a door or a window? That's what you firemen do, right?"

"Yeah," he draws out, as if the word stretches into the next century.

"Why do I get the feeling you lost the thread of the conversation and you're staring at my boobs instead?"

Shedding his bathrobe, he steps into the tub as well. "Because I was. Because you're fucking distracting. You're naked and hot as hell. I can't think about fireman stuff. I can't think about anything but getting my hands on you again."

That's all I want too.

Once wasn't enough to curb my desire for him. Once, as magnificent as that one time was, barely scratched the surface. As I sink into the decadently hot water that bubbles around us, he glides over to me, wraps his arms around my waist, and drops a delicious kiss to my lips.

I murmur, my eyes fluttering closed, goosebumps rising on my flesh.

This time, his kiss is soft, an exploration. Like he's taking the time to get to know my mouth, my lips, my jaw. His lips skate over mine, travel across my face as if he's marking me with kisses—with mind-bending kisses. I scoot closer, my wet, naked body pressed to him.

He slides his hands up my back, into my hair, then down again, cupping my ass. "You're spectacular."

My fingers have goals of their own, and they travel along his chest, across his shoulders, down his strong arms, tracing his muscles. "So are you." I stop at the jagged white scar cutting from his stomach to his right hip. "I noticed this in the calendar."

"You were looking at my calendar page?"

"Of course. You're the hottest."

"Damn straight."

"Is it from work?"

He nods. "Fire at a winery. A beam fell. Hit me and ripped some skin."

I wince. "Ouch."

He shrugs like it was nothing. "I'm tough."

"I know. But I want you to be careful." My voice sounds tender, and that's the truth of how I feel for him. Even if this is a one-night-only thing—and I don't know why it would be more—I want him safe and happy and well. "Your job has risks."

He grins like that's the best thing I could have said. "I am safe. And I'm careful. I promise."

"Good. I don't want anything happening to you."

His grin stretches. "You want me sticking around, V?"

I punch him lightly. "Yes, stick around, please."

His smile possibly reaches the sky. "I'll do my best." After sinking onto one of the seats in the tub, he tugs me on top of him so I straddle his legs.

"And now this hot tub is getting red-hot."

"Please. It's *white*-hot."

He hums a dirty little ditty, then his expression shifts to serious. "In there," he says, tipping his forehead to the cabin, "I meant everything I said." His eyes are etched with honesty and a vulnerability that reaches into my chest and grabs hold of my heart, squeezing it tightly. The way he looks at me makes me want to run inside, call Perri, and ask for forgiveness and then permission, because this man is all I want.

But this isn't about her right now. Because I don't know that Shaw wants the same things I do. If he doesn't—and I still have no reason to think he does—Perri doesn't need my confession. Not if tonight is all there is.

Oh, but if he does want the same things . . .

He is, at the very least, worth testing the waters.

"What do you mean?" I ask, hope wrapping around me.

With the pad of his thumb, he strokes my chin. "I've wanted you for so damn long. I've wanted to kiss you, I swear, since . . ."

My heart somersaults. He's so close to voicing what I feel, something worth rocking the boat with my best friend. "Since when?"

He gazes at me, stroking my arms, threading his hands in my hair. "I can't stop touching you. I just can't."

"Don't stop, then."

Curling a big hand around the back of my head, he draws me in for another kiss. My skin tingles, and pleasure tightens in me, swirling in my core.

"Since high school," he answers when he breaks the kiss. "High school and college and ever since."

I smile a big, dopey grin. "Same here."

"Yeah?"

"Absolutely."

I seal my mouth to his, kissing him in a tender, gentle way I hope intoxicates him like he's done to me.

He sweeps his tongue over mine, and we're both melting into each other. We kiss for long minutes, the jets of the hot tub hitting us, the bubbles jamming out their own background soundtrack, the snow tumbling from the sky. I'm falling, too, under the spell of tonight. Falling far. Falling hard.

"What took us so long to do this?" he asks when we stop.

This.

I need to remember what *this* is.

I can't fall harder. I need to fall *out*.

Right now, we are only passing the time. This is a plan to get him out of my system. To eradicate all my wild emotions so I can walk away and finally stop comparing other men to him.

I'm having him, so I can move on from him.

But it feels so good to tell him what I want. "Maybe because a certain someone didn't want us to," I tease.

Laughing, he sets a finger to my lips. "Don't say her name. It's just you and me tonight."

And that reminds me yet again that *this* is for tonight. So I'll take tonight. I run my hands through his damp hair. "By the way, I presume you're spending the night."

He laughs, tossing his head back. "You're not kicking me out now, snow bunny. The roads are closed, the snow isn't stopping, and I don't even have any service on my cell."

"You need a cell to drive?"

"I need a cell if there's a problem. I'm a fireman. We're trained to deal with emergencies, and I find it best if we don't cause any, but should I encounter any, I want to be prepared. A working cell helps."

I wiggle my eyebrows. "Well, you can put out the fires here, then."

He gazes appreciatively at me as he slides his hands along my thighs. "You got a fire I need to extinguish?"

I dip my hand between his legs and squeeze his erection. "I think we both do."

He groans, his eyelids hooded. "Fuck, that's good."

I bury my face in his neck, kissing my way to his ear. "Want to pass the time again?"

"Hell, yeah."

I rub against him, kissing him, getting us both so worked up we're groaning and gasping, and I'm sure the deer and woodland creatures are cringing and covering their ears in embarrassment.

But before we do it in the water, I set my hands on his chest. "Hot tubs are great, but I'd really like to get you in my mouth, and also not drown nor have you freeze."

"Enough said."

Seconds later, we've grabbed our clothes and keys, scurried inside, and locked the door behind us. I tell him to sit on the couch in front of the fireplace.

With the fire warming my skin, I drop down to my knees and take his cock in my hand, savoring the velvety steel of his length. He jerks against me, my name like a dirty prayer on his lips.

One firm stroke and I let go and dip my head between his legs. I wrap my lips around his shaft, taking him in deep.

"Fuck, Vanessa," he says, and his hands dart into my hair.

Drawing him in, I thrill at the wonderful reality. This man is mine tonight.

He's resplendent like this, with his thick, strong legs spread, his big arms around my head, his body slouched into the couch. I cup his balls, toying with them as I suck.

He tastes so damn good because it's him. As I bring him to the back of my throat, he grunts, making the dirtiest sounds. Then he thrusts hard, nearly making me gag.

In a split second, he stops, yanks me up, and stares at me with wild, dirty eyes. "Get on my face while you do that."

"Really?"

"Yes." He slides down so he's flat on the couch. "I need to eat this pussy while you suck me dry."

A spark ignites in me, lit in my core and spiraling through my body from his filthy words. "I've never sixty-nined," I admit.

He blinks. "No?"

"Never."

He sighs, like a satisfied man. "That's fucking awesome. That's the hottest thing anyone has ever said to me. I'm going to come so hard, baby. You okay with that?"

I smile sheepishly. "I think I'll like it."

He slides me around, tugging me to his face so I'm practically draped on him. At the first flick of his tongue, I groan like an animal.

"Oh God," I breathe out, and he moans too, licking me as I return his cock to my mouth.

He spreads my legs wider, lapping me up as I draw him back into me. It's heady and dirty, the way we are, draped over each other's bodies, lavishing dizzying attention with tongues and mouths and now ... fingers.

Oh God. Dear Lord.

I shudder, my entire body shaking as pleasure kaleidoscopes through me from his mouth, his tongue, and his fingers fucking me.

Everything, every damn thing about this moment is so intense, so erotic.

So *intimate*.

Is it insane to feel closer to him right now than when we were fucking? I'm not looking in his eyes. He's staring at my ass, if he's even looking. Hell, my mouth is full of his thick, hard cock, but with his groans and my sounds and the wildness, I feel closer. So close that pleasure tightens in my belly.

I can't keep him in my mouth. I let go, his cock falling from my lips, as I give in to the storm inside me, to the swirl of sensations, to the burst of pleasure.

Over and over, it builds from his tongue licking me, caressing me, his fingers in me and on me and spreading me, and it's like he's fucking me with his mouth and his hands at the same time.

And his sounds.

The noises he makes are lustful, carnal moans that tell me he loves doing this to me.

And I love what he's doing so damn much that the desire pulses between my legs and the exquisite ache ramps up until finally I climb to the heavens, soaring in ecstasy, babbling, shouting, crying out.

I'm incoherent as I come ridiculously hard on his face.

And before I know it, he's spinning me around, hunting for another condom, but I shake my head. "Clean, I'm clean. Are you?"

"Tested. Yes," he grunts, and that's enough.

I sink down on him.

"Shaw," I groan in ecstasy as he fills me.

"Vanessa," he says, and it sounds like a plea.

"That was the most intense orgasm of my life," I murmur as I rise up then drop back down, grinding on his fantastic dick.

He grabs my hips, moving me quickly. "You're so

fucking sexy when you come. So fucking sexy all the time. So fucking sexy now."

His fingers dig into me. His hands grip me. And he fucks up into me, harder, wilder. He grunts and growls, teetering near the edge.

"I want you to come, baby," I tell him, sliding my chest against his.

He groans.

"Don't hold out for me. I'm good. I want you to."

He grabs the back of my head, yanking me in for a fierce kiss. "You're perfect. God, I'm so crazy for you."

And his words, they ring in my ears. They're like a song. They're like bells announcing my dreams.

They're the best thing I've ever heard. The man I love is crazy for me. And I'm so damn crazy for him that hearing that sends me on a fast track to pleasure.

"Say it again," I tell him.

"Does it turn you on?"

"So much."

He slams me hard onto him. "I'm fucking crazy for you."

I pant. "I'm crazy for you."

I close my eyes, riding him, riding us to the edge of pleasure, till the bliss grabs me and pulls me under. I come, and he comes, and we come together.

After, he wraps an arm around me and sighs

contentedly. "I'm pretty sure that was the best sex ever in the world."

"It definitely was. Nobody does it better," I whisper.

"That's for damn sure. Nobody does it better than us."

And I know why. Because of what I feel for him, and what I hope he feels for me.

Sex makes me hungry.

We eat the sandwiches I picked up earlier.

We play Monopoly for a few minutes, and he shows me how well he can juggle the tiny shoe, the iron, and the car.

I clap like a pleased spectator at the circus. I have always been a Shaw enabler.

I wait for him to say those words. *I'm crazy for you.*

I want to hear him say it again when we're not in the heat of the moment.

But I also want this moment to last as long as it can.

When he takes me to bed, we go again, and I hope those words will fall from his lips as he puts me on my hands and knees, then afterward as he draws me into his arms, curling his strong body around mine.

I suppose I could say it too. I'm an equal-opportunity gal. And I'm dying to know if tonight was the real deal or a one-time thing.

But asking will change things either way, and I'm not ready for this moment to end. So I stay silent on matters of the heart all through the night.

When I rise, the light of the new day shines on the man in bed next to me. As sunbeams dance across his sleeping form, the realization deepens.

This is what I want.

Waking up with Shaw. Every day.

And to get what you want, you need to ask for it.

As I kick off the covers, I resolve to tell him how I feel. I resolve, too, to talk to Perri and see how she'd truly feel if I dated her brother. While she's made her stance clear in the past, she also loves me and wants me to be happy. Surely if she knows how happy I am with him, she'll be supportive.

I always bring a change of clothes when I come to Tahoe, so I tug on yoga pants and a sweatshirt, brush my teeth, and then pad to the kitchen, resolved to move forward and figure out what we can be.

The snow has stopped, the air is crisp, and it's a brand-new day. I whip up some eggs and toast.

When I catch a glimpse of the clock, I see it's nearly eleven.

"Holy cow. We really slept in," I murmur.

When the eggs are done, I hear the shuffle of feet, a yawn, and a stretch. I turn around to where one seriously sleep-rumpled, sexy man wanders into the kitchen wearing only boxer briefs.

"Hey, you," I say.

"Hey, you."

But the next sound we hear isn't either one of us.

It's my best friend. Because she's banging on the cabin door.

12

SHAW

I came to this cabin seeking answers. The next morning, I have all of them. Every single last one.

I know exactly why I don't want Vanessa to go to the wedding with someone else.

Because I don't want Vanessa to go to any wedding at any time with any other man. Or on any other date. I want to be the one on her arm now and always.

So, yeah, we had great sex. Duh.

Given how long I've wanted her, that's no surprise. But the sex was also amazing because I *finally* understand why I've wanted her with such ferocity. Light bulbs popped, bells rang, birds sang, and chimes chimed. Freaking angels crooned from the heavens.

I'm in love with her.

That means I need to take care of a few important matters, stat.

Like taking a leak.

Hey, nature calls.

I head to the bathroom, drain the dragon, wash my hands, and brush my teeth.

On to the next critical matter.

Tell the woman I love her, hope to God she feels the same, then figure out how to break the news to the she-ogre that is my sister when it comes to Vanessa.

The scent of scrambled eggs and coffee wafts through the cabin, and I walk into the kitchen in my skivvies, sporting a new round of morning wood—or maybe it's just Vanessa wood. I plan to slink my arms around the brunette beauty, kiss her neck, inhale her sexy scent, and tell her I meant every word last night.

Every word and more.

Instead, someone knocks wildly on the door, before Vanessa yanks it open.

My dick crawls back into my body, curls up and hides under a couch.

Stationed in the doorway is one wildly worried leprechaun, stomping her feet, flapping her hands. "I thought you were dead! I was calling you all night.

And all morning." Perri points at Vanessa as she goes full j'accuse in a court of law. I don't think she's seen me yet. But she must have noticed my truck.

"Why would I be dead?" Vanessa asks, and I can hear the deflection in her voice, and the nerves too.

"Because of the snow! It was terrible, and I was worried about you, and you didn't answer your phone. And Shaw didn't either. I thought you were both dead."

"There's no service here! And why was I supposed to text you? You knew where I was."

Perri's eyes bug out, her neck shooting forward like a peacock pecking. "Because! Because I worry. Hello! I'm the girl who raced to the hospital in college when you broke your leg. I tried the landline too."

Vanessa's brow knits. "There's a landline?"

Perri huffs. "You gave me the number in college. Did you forget?"

"Yes! Maybe I forgot that we had one, but it never rang, so it might not even be on or plugged in or whatever the hell you do with landlines. Did you really think I was dead?"

Perri's voice shoots to Saturn. "*Yes.* And as soon as the snow cleared this morning, I got in my car and drove up to see if you were. Derek came with me. I was worried. That's who I am. I'm the worrier because I've seen too much every day in my job."

She waves behind her as footsteps crunch in the snow. Derek trudges up the steps, thumbs hooked in the loops of his jeans.

He tips his chin at me. "Hey, man."

"Hey."

Perri snaps her gaze to me, and her jaw hits the floor in shocked surprise. She stumbles back, grabbing the doorjamb.

"What the what?" she sputters, as she widens her eyes at my attire, such that it is. "Why are you in your boxers?" She whips her head to Vanessa—"Why is my brother in his boxers?"—and back to me. "You were supposed to be helping her with the cabin, not doing a striptease."

"I helped, and we spent the night," I say, since there's no point lying about that. It's motherfucking obvious. "We spent it together."

Vanessa parts her lips, nibbles on the corner, her eyes widening with guilt. I wonder if I spoke too soon. If we were supposed to lie. But fuck it, I don't want to lie about my feelings for her anymore.

Perri squeezes her eyes shut, as if she's snow-blind, then opens them. "Are you two . . . ?"

She can't even finish.

My heart nose-dives, my chest has an elephant in it, and my gut feels like I ate bad chili.

While I don't feel a snick of guilt for spending the

night with Vanessa, I do feel a ton of it for going against Perri's wishes.

Even if I don't agree with them.

Because I should have told her first. I should have told her how I feel. My sister is crazy and intense, but I love and respect her, and the look in her eyes screams her abject disappointment in me.

Though that's nothing compared to the gaze she casts Vanessa. My sister's green eyes are now the color of hurt. "Are you guys—"

She seems to be at a loss for words.

Vanessa reaches for Perri's arm, her voice breaking as she tries to reassure her. "It's not what you think."

I step in the middle of things, sweeping over to the open door. "It's freezing outside. Just come in."

Vanessa ushers the visitors inside, cold swirling in with them like a trailing perfume. Once the door shuts, my sister stares at me, and she's no longer shocked, or even surprised. She's hurt. Just plain hurt. Tears, a mere hint, flicker in her eyes.

"Are you guys together?" she whispers, like she can't believe we didn't tell her first.

I lick my lips and look at Vanessa. She gazes back at me. This isn't how I wanted to tell her I've fallen in love with her. I spoke first before so maybe I ought to wait for Vanessa to answer.

But before either of us can reply, Perri shifts again to a frown. "Shaw. I've told you to stay away."

I snap.

That's all it takes. "Why the hell am I not good enough for your friend?"

Just like when we were younger, Perri gives it right back to me. "Are you for real? You're standing here in your boxer shorts. That's why. If you were going to do right by her, you wouldn't be half naked. You'd be dating her. You'd be taking her out. You'd have told me how you felt. Now can you please get dressed, because I can't have this conversation with you flapping around in your underwear."

"We're not done with this," I mutter.

I retreat to the bedroom, with Derek following behind, trying to figure out how to unmake this mess.

13

VANESSA

I sink onto the couch, and my first instinct is to say I'm sorry. But I believe that women say they're sorry too often and for the wrong things. We say we're sorry for our life choices, for asking for help, for our sexuality, when we should only apologize for the things we've actually done to hurt someone else.

I've hurt Perri.

As she slumps onto the cushions, wiping a rebel tear from her cheek, I try to take ownership for my wrongs.

"I'm sorry this is how you found out about my feelings for him. And I'm sorry I didn't tell you sooner, but if I was going to, I'd have told you years ago that I'm in love with your brother."

Slowly, as if this moment were unfolding in a jar of molasses, she turns to meet my gaze. "For years?"

Her voice is quiet, but each word is clear. Like she's testing the full weight of them.

Relief overwhelms me, flooding my heart. Telling her tastes like freedom. "Since high school. You probably think it's crazy. Maybe it is crazy. And the thing I feel worst about is I kept it a secret from you. I love you so much, and you and Arden are my best friends, and that's why it tore me apart at times to know I had these intense feelings for your brother." I feel lighter already. "But yes, I've felt this way for him for a long, long time."

She swallows. "You're really in love with him, and have been since he was a cocky, mouthy, corny, class-clown-meets-jock high school guy?"

"You're such a sister," I say with a little laugh.

"But he was," she insists. "He was all of those things."

"And he made me laugh. And we had fun. And yes, I'm really in love with him, and love makes you do crazy things, like go for it with a guy. Like drive two hours for a friend when you can't get through on her cell phone, right?"

"That was reasonable. You could have been dead, remember? Besides, I'm a cop. That's what I do. Make sure my people are safe."

"Like I said. Love is crazy. And love makes you do things like keep a secret because you want to protect this person you love." I reach for her hand, squeezing it, needing her to know she's my person too. "I wanted to protect you because I knew you'd worry about me. You always have."

She tightens her hold on my hand, and the look in her eyes is so fierce. "Because I love you like you're family. Because I want the world for you. Don't you get that?"

My throat tightens. "I do, I totally understand it. And I want the same for you. I wanted it for you when you were falling for Derek. I want you to have everything. I understand why you do what you do. I understand why you haven't wanted this to happen." I shrug helplessly. "But my heart's been his for a long time. For years."

She nods as if she's trying to absorb all this new intel. "Why didn't you tell me?"

I give her an arched eyebrow of disbelief. "Seriously?" I nudge her elbow. "Who's the crazy one? You'd have cackled. Said he's not good enough for me, even though he's your freaking brother."

She straightens, her nostrils flaring. "But he's *not* good enough for you. Yes, he's a great brother. Yes, he's a great guy. And yes, if I were in trouble, he's the one I'd call. Well, before I met Derek." Perri takes a beat, her voice softening to a worried whisper. "But he's not a committed type of guy. He's a ladies' man. You want something real. How can he give it to you?"

I draw a deep breath, wishing I had the answer. But I do know I won't find it in Perri.

The answer is in my heart.

And in Shaw's, if he wants what I have to give.

"I do want something real, and I want that to be with Shaw. I'm willing to take that chance. I haven't been able to get him out of my heart or my mind for years. And yes, I slept with him last night, and I'm not going to apologize for that. And I'm not going to apologize for enjoying it."

She pretends to retch. "No more details, please. I'm begging you."

I hold up my hands in surrender. "I won't give you any more details."

"Please never do."

And because I can't resist needling her, I whisper, "But it was amazing."

She slams her hands over her ears. "La la la la la."

I peel them off. "But I am sorry I kept my feelings a secret from you and that I didn't talk to you before this happened. Except . . . maybe it needed to happen this way. Maybe Shaw and I needed to be forced together to confront how we feel. And maybe I needed to have this chance with him without involving you. So I could do it for me. Learn for me. Discover if what I felt from afar was true up close too."

She hums as if she's thinking about all of this. "Do you know how he feels for you?"

Nerves fly through my body, chased by wishes and hopes. "I don't know, but I have a good idea, and I hope I'm right. He said he's crazy about me."

"He said he's crazy about you?"

Smiling, I feel a little giddy at the memory. *Crazy for you* isn't love, but surely it's a start. It's something to build on. "I'm willing to take a chance."

"But what if it doesn't work out? What happens to us?" she asks, and that's when I understand Perri's biggest concern. *Us.* Somehow, this crazy loon thinks a man could ruin our friendship.

I scoff and laugh at the same time. "Do you really think we're not going to be friends if it doesn't work out?"

"Yes. He's my brother. I can't change that fact. And what if it doesn't work out and you're done with me by extension?"

Cracking up, I rap my knuckles on her temple. "You're insane. You're not getting rid of me so easily. No matter what, we're still friends, and that's not going to change."

She exhales deeply, and her remaining hard edges seem to soften. "I don't want him to hurt you. If he does, I will have his you-know-what in a sling."

"I don't want him to hurt me either, but I also don't want to spend the rest of my life wondering what might've happened with him. I don't want to compare other men to him. I want to know if we can be what I want us to be. And I want your blessing."

A tear rolls down her cheek. "All I want is for you to be happy. If that big idiot makes you happy, go for it."

I couldn't be happier right now. I love my friend so damn much. I throw my arms around her and pull her in for a hug. We both cry. They're not tears of sadness. They're tears of letting go of the one thing that stood between us.

The floorboards creak.

We separate, and I turn to see Shaw and Derek entering the living room. Shaw's dressed now, wearing jeans and his sweater from yesterday. Looks like he's dragged his fingers through his hair to comb it.

He clears his throat. "So, there's something I want to tell you, Vanessa." His eyes swim with hope and vulnerability.

But I speak first, saying out loud words I've held inside me for so long. "I'm in love with you."

14

SHAW

Derek glares. "Just tell her, man."

"Vanessa?" I raise an eyebrow as I tug on my sweater.

He leans against the door of the bedroom. "Yes. But in this case, I mean *my* bride. Tell Perri you're going to do right by her friend. That's all she needs to know. I assure you."

"You assure me?"

"Trust me. No one knows her better than I do. Now, get out there, get your woman, and sort it out with your sister."

My woman.

That's the answer I've been searching for.

When it comes to Vanessa, I don't want what I can't have. I don't want a one-night fling. I don't want a friendship.

I want all of her for all of me.

It's now. I'm telling her.

I leave the bedroom, run my fingers through my hair, and head down the hall. I'm going for it completely. Nothing is going to stop me.

Not even her when she spots me.

"I'm in love with you."

Nope. Nothing is stopping me. Not even the best words anyone has ever said to me. Words that touch down in my heart and burrow inside it, making me so damn happy. I'm a man on a mission.

I stride across the living room, reach for Vanessa's hand, pull her up from the couch, and wrap my arms around her. "I'm in love with you too."

She melts against me, warm and snuggly and wonderful. I press a kiss to her hair. "I think I have been for a long, long time."

Somewhere behind me I swear I hear Derek murmur, "*I fucking knew it.*"

I ignore him because Vanessa looks up at me with a huge goofy grin on her face. "Same here," she says. "It's been since high school for me."

I feel like I'm made of gold. "Is that so?"

She loops her arms around my neck. "What can I say? I had a crush, and it never stopped."

Perri clears her throat, and I let go of Vanessa but take her hand in mine as I turn to my not-a-banshee-anymore sibling. "Perri, I love you like a sister."

She rolls her eyes.

"And I never went for it with Vanessa because I respected your wishes. But here's the thing." I look her straight in the eyes. "You might think I'm not serious, but that's because I save it for work. I save it for my job. I save it for when I have to save lives—just like you do."

Perri sighs but then nods, and I know she understands me deeply. On this, we've always connected. She's a cop, I'm a fireman—and we both do what we do to help others.

"I need a little levity outside of work. That's why I make jokes, keep it light. You get me?"

"I do," she says softly.

"So you might not see that side of me, but I have it. I have it when I walk into burning buildings. When I answer heart attack calls in the middle of the night. When we rush to an accident on the highway. Same as you."

"I understand."

"And the other thing I don't joke about is this woman." I squeeze Vanessa's hand harder and turn to face her. "I fucking love you so much. So much that you simply can't go to the wedding with Jamie. You're going with me."

Vanessa laughs. "You're not asking? You're telling me?"

I roll my eyes. "Woman, you're going with me, you want to, and that's that."

She grins, smacking my chest. "Fine. If you insist."

I look back at Perri. "Cancel Jamie. Call off that blind date. Whatever you need to do. Vanessa is mine, and I'm a hundred percent serious about that. And you need to know I will treat her right; I will do right by her. I will treat her like the queen she is to me. So you can just stop worrying and talking shit about my balls."

Perri's mouth parts in an offended O. "I do not want to discuss your balls. Now or ever."

I grab my crotch. "Good. The balls are off-limits. And so is Vanessa. No more setups. No more anything." I drape my arm around my woman, tug her closer, and plant a quick kiss on her lips. "She's taken."

Perri's smile is huge and surprises the hell out of me. She jumps up and wraps her arms around both of us. "I love you guys. Just be good to each other. Always, okay? Or I'll hunt you down and break your arm, Shaw."

I laugh. "It's always something with you, isn't it?"

"Always," Perri adds.

The three of us separate, and I return to the final matter at hand. "You're going to uninvite Jamie now?"

Perri furrows her brow. "He's a guest. That'd be rude."

"Then uninvite him from the blind date."

Vanessa chimes in. "I should let Miriam know too. It's the right thing to do."

Derek coughs, cutting in. "I can handle that."

I turn and stare at him quizzically. So does Vanessa. And Perri.

He shrugs, an impish grin on his face. "I might have played a part in the whole thing."

15

DEREK

Sometimes you have to take chances.

Last year, I took a chance to be with Perri.

And this past week, I took a chance for Shaw.

Even though there were risks. Like pissing off the woman I love.

Perri marches up to me, slams her hands on my chest, and quietly hisses, "What did you do?"

But I'm not worried. I know how to smooth things over with this fiery woman I adore to the ends of the Earth and back. I smile and run a hand through her hair. "Kitten, it's all good. I knew he was in love with her."

She squints. "How did you know that? I didn't know that."

I scoff. "You didn't want to know that! But I've been trying to tell you for months. He's so damn crazy about Vanessa. I could barely handle him mooning over her every time he saw her."

"So you did what exactly? Arranged a snowstorm?"

I wiggle my eyebrows, pleased at my machinations. "I'm good, but I'm not that good."

Her eyes don't let go of mine. "So what did you do, McBride? Don't make me cuff you and bring you in for questioning."

I loop my arm around her waist and raise my eyebrows. "That might not be so bad. But you won't, because I'm not the bad guy in this story. There is no bad guy. I'm one of the good guys, and I did a good thing for everyone by making all this love happen."

"And how did you do that, Mr. Matchmaker?"

I smile, pleased as the dickens. "I talked to Miriam at the library when I was there with my niece. We chatted about a bunch of things. Her son, Vanessa, Shaw, and oh yeah, someone else."

"Who?"

I whisper in her ear.

"What?" Shock covers Perri's face when she draws back.

"Indeed. And look, Vanessa and Shaw needed a kick in the pants to get together. So I gave them one."

"What if it had gone south?"

"But it didn't. Because we engineered it brilliantly. And besides, these two," I say, gesturing to the new lovebirds, "are so in love that it simply couldn't go wrong. So Miriam and I arranged the whole Jamie-Vanessa thing to get the two of them moving. It worked. I knew Shaw would only get his butt in gear if someone serious seemed to be going after Vanessa. I also knew she was crazy about him." I run my fingers over Perri's cheek, giving a smile just for her. "And I knew you'd forgive me."

She breathes out hard. "That's a lot of assumptions."

"But you forgive me?"

"Hmm." She's softening. "Why should I?"

"Because I pushed all the right buttons to engineer true love."

She turns to look at Shaw and Vanessa, who seem sickeningly happy, then she turns back to me. "Fine. I forgive you."

"Good, because I fucking love you, and I also knew you'd be happy if Vanessa was finally with the man she wanted."

Perri sighs contentedly. "She does seem to like him."

I shift my gaze to the hallway. "How many bedrooms does this cabin have?"

"At least two, I think."

"What do you say we claim one for the rest of the day?"

"I'd say that's a deal."

* * *

Shaw

Later, we tromp outside in the snow for a snowball fight, and the ladies make snow angels as the sun shines brightly on a carpet of white.

With my phone, I snap a picture of my very own snow bunny, then I tug her up from the ground and press a kiss to her cold nose.

"Hey, you," I whisper. "So this is kind of nice."

She stares down the bridge of her nose. "Kind of?"

I shrug nonchalantly. "Kind of totally fucking awesome." Then I sniff. "Also, it smells like juniper out here."

"That's the juniper tree," she says, waving behind her toward a thatch of trees. "And thanks a lot. Now I'm craving a juniper latte."

I hold up one finger. "I promised to treat you like a queen. Be right back."

I grab Derek, take off in my truck on the newly plowed road, and return a little later with a quartet of juniper lattes.

"Told you I'd treat her right," I say to Perri as I hand the beverage to my woman.

Vanessa taps her fingernail against the side of the cup. "This is pretty good treatment."

That evening, over a simple dinner and snacks, the four of us play Monopoly, then we go to our separate rooms. All I will say is thank God they're on opposite ends of the cabin.

Because Vanessa and I make use of ours.

All. Night. Long.

16

BOOK CLUB LADIES GROUP CHAT

Miriam: Everything is in place. All systems are go. Fingers crossed for liftoff.

CarolAnn: Toes crossed too!

Miriam: I have faith in our matchmaking. It's going to go perfectly. It's not like there's anyone else in the picture. We have this all mapped out. Don't forget that, ladies.

Sara: Plus, we're damn good at this. Look at Hunter and Madeline, already hitting it off. Surely we'll be two for two.

Miriam: By the way, I am so glad we added secret matchmaking to our book club responsibilities.

CarolAnn: So am I. And we are quite amazing at it, if I do say so myself. Then again, we're grand at so many things: book clubbing, wine drinking, not to mention NSFW conversating.

Sara: We do rule at all those over-sixty hobbies.

Miriam: Ladies, let's agree we get better with age.

CarolAnn: We are the finest of fine wines.

Sara: Have I mentioned that retirement is officially the most awesome part of our lives?

CarolAnn: I'll drink a merlot to that!

Miriam: Let's keep making things happen. The wedding is going to be fantastic. You're the best friends a gal could have.

Sara: Cheers to us!

Miriam: And to the young people who benefit from a nudge here and there. May they be blessed with love, trust, and the hottest of hot sex.

CarolAnn: Double cheers to that.

Sara: Make mine a triple. :)

EPILOGUE

Vanessa

In his tux, Shaw is exactly as handsome as I imagined he'd look.

Correction: more handsome. He's somehow even better-looking now that he's mine. Because we've opened up to each other. Because we trust each other. Because we're together, and that makes me more attracted to him every single day.

Crazy, huh? I already thought I'd reached the edge of attraction, but I can see that it's infinite when you don't have to love in secret. I love Shaw more now that I've set my emotions free from where I'd hidden them—free with room to breathe and expand and grow.

I love him more now that I can share my love with him.

With his elbow hooked through mine, we walk down the aisle till we reach Derek and the minister, who happens to be married to Derek's sister. His brother-in-law is a military chaplain, so he's handling the vows.

Shaw takes his place next to the groom, his smile lingering on me. I stand next to Arden, and Derek's sister, Jodie. When the wedding music begins, all eyes turn to the bride as Perri, radiant in white and holding a bouquet of lilies, walks down the aisle, looking as happy as anyone could ever possibly be on her wedding day. When she reaches the altar, she meets Derek's gaze and whispers *hi*.

It's so tender and intimate. It's everything I could want for my friend.

He whispers *hi* back to her, and even in that two-letter word, I hear so much love. My throat catches, and out of the corner of my eye, I glance at Arden next to me. We don't have to say anything. We've always had an intuitive kind of language, the three of us friends. I feel passing between us this happiness—this awareness that here we are, decades later, still best friends and heading into new and wonderfully fabulous phases of our lives.

* * *

Later, the three of us gather in a corner of the reception hall under the twinkling lights, watching other guests dance. I lift a glass of champagne to offer a toast. "Look at us. The kick-ass girls of Lucky Falls."

Perri raises a glass high. "I propose a new name. The kick-ass women."

Arden lifts her champagne but doesn't take a drink. "I'll toast to that."

I stare at her, instantly knowing why the bubbly isn't touching her lips. "Why aren't you drinking champagne? Is there something you want to tell us?"

She giggles then says, "I'm having a baby in six more months."

I squeal. Perri shrieks. And we group-hug in the biggest group hug ever.

Someone else is having a good time here too.

My little sister.

Turns out Ella's the one Miriam had in mind for Jamie.

Turns out Jamie has had his eye on her for a while as well.

And all it took was Derek and Miriam plotting to bring two new couples together.

The other night, I texted her.

Vanessa: Why didn't you tell me YOU were the one who wanted to get on Jamie, stat?

Ella: I did say he deserved a Marquez sister. I just didn't say which one. :)

Vanessa: My, my. You sure do like semantics, don't you?

Ella: I do enjoy words. :) But seriously. I also knew you'd never wind up with him.

Vanessa: Why?

Ella: Please. I'm a lover of books, stories, and romance. I've been devouring tales since I could read. It was inevitable that you had it bad for your best friend's brother, and it would only take time, or a snowstorm, for you to get together. I wish I could take responsibility for that snowstorm, but fate obviously knew the two of you needed it.

Vanessa: You're too observant for your own good.

Ella: Well, it was patently obvious you've had it bad for Shaw for years.

Vanessa: And do you have it bad for Jamie?

Ella: I haven't even been on a date with him!

Vanessa: That's not the question.

Ella: I'll answer the question after I go out with him.

Vanessa: My money is on yes.

I take a spin on the dance floor with Shaw, passing Ella and Jamie on the way. He looks enchanted with my sexy librarian sister. I wink and wish her luck.

She blows me a kiss. "Your money is right."

"I knew it."

On the other side of the room, Miriam tucks a strand of hair behind her ear and smiles. Shaw and I make our way across the dance floor, stopping in front of her.

"Thank you, Miriam."

"No, darling. Thank you. All is well in Lucky Falls when it comes to love."

"I'll say."

We return to dancing, where we shimmy next to Shaw's father and mother. His dad gives a tip of the cap, a nod, and a smile to his son, then mouths *Well done.*

"I'll say," Shaw echoes.

ANOTHER EPILOGUE

Shaw

Several months later

I check the weather report. There's a snowstorm coming in, and I have the weekend off. So does my girlfriend.

I head to her bowling alley for a few rounds, then a few not-so-stolen kisses, then tell her I plan to take her to Tahoe the next day. "No ifs, ands, or buts about it."

She gives me a look. "Like I was going to protest? You drive, I'll play Elvis on the Bluetooth, and I'll bring those sexy sweaters that get you revved up."

"Everything you do gets me revved up."

We drive up together, listening to fifties tunes

about love and Cupid. She teaches me a few more Spanish phrases. I've been picking up bits and pieces of the language. Well, beyond the ones I hear most frequently—*oh Shaw, yes Shaw, my God, do it again*, and *more, more, more.*

In town, we stop at the market and pick up food, beer, champagne, and all the fixings for hot chocolate.

At the cabin, she says she'll straighten up the bedroom, and while she does, I start a fire and whip up some hot chocolate, adding a dollop of whipped cream to each mug.

"Well, don't you know the way to my heart and panties," she says when she returns to the living room.

I stand in front of the fireplace, a cup in each hand. "I'd like to keep finding my way there for the rest of our lives."

She tilts her head curiously. "What do you mean?"

And as soon as I hand her a mug, setting mine down on the table, I drop to one knee.

"Yes!"

I burst out in laughter. "You didn't even let me ask!"

She clasps her hands over her mouth. "Yes!"

"I'm asking anyway," I say through my chuckles. I straighten out my smile because this is a time to be serious. "Vanessa Marquez, you are all my answers, and I love you so much. You're my snow bunny, my friend, my lover, and the only woman I ever want to come home to after a fire. I want to be yours forever, and I want you to be mine."

She shouts *yes* again as tears streak down her face.

"Maybe take a look at your hot chocolate," I say, nodding to her snowman mug.

On the handle, I've strung a diamond ring.

Her eyes widen. "Oh my God. It's gorgeous."

I untie it, slide it onto her finger, and kiss her in front of the fire as the snow begins to fall.

BONUS EPILOGUE

The Kick-ass Women of Lucky Falls Group Chat (plus Ella)

Arden: It's official!

Perri: It's official, as in you actually went into the hospital and became a mother, and we're just learning now? I'm on my way. Lights and sirens!

Arden: Please. In that case, I would've called Gabe, and then called you, and then yelled at you, as well as at Gabe, J. K. Rowling, Stephen King, Shakespeare, God, and everyone else during labor.

Vanessa: Good to know you include us worthy of shouting at, along with literary giants, while pushing a watermelon or two out of you. So . . . what's official, then? You're finally going to take a few weeks off and rest before you give birth, like you really should be doing, you naughty, naughty girl who keeps on working well past when she's supposed to?

Arden: No. I've officially become a house. It happened today. I tried to bend over and practically fell to the floor. That means I'm a house.

Perri: I was thinking an apartment building. But all kidding aside, you really need to be careful, sweetie. We can't have you toppling over.

Ella: Yes, because if you toppled over, I'm pretty sure we'd have to come roll you out of your home, right?

Vanessa: Oh, you are getting sassy, Ella.

Ella: Wasn't that the requirement when you invited me into your group chat? Be as sassy as I can possibly be?

Vanessa: I have taught you so well. I'm so proud of you for trying to keep up.

Ella: I do more than keep up.

Arden: Hello, tangent AF. Doesn't anyone feel sorry for me? I'm colonial-home-size, you're going to be rolling me across the floor like a beached whale, and we're discussing Ella's banter skills. Is there no sympathy for my condition?

Perri: I'm sympathetic and yet practical. Do you have any idea how hard beached whales are to move? We need a plan. We might have to call the fire department.

Arden: Well, it's one member of the fire department's fault that I'm this size!

Ella: *clears throat* Excuse me, but I think you might have been involved in that decision too.

Arden: And I regret nothing, but I'm becoming the Queen Mary. This has to be Gabe's fault for giving me twins.

Perri: Uh, to point out the obvious, your genes dictate twins, not his. Also, you have twins on your side of the family.

Arden: I know that, but it feels like he's responsible for my gigantism! CAN SOMEONE JUST BE SYMPATHETIC, PLEASE?????

Vanessa: I'm trying, but I'm too excited every time I think about the fact that you're going to pop out two babies. In fact, I'm going shopping right now for more baby gifts for you.

Perri: Pink baby gifts!!! I'll join you!

Ella: Pink matching sets of stuff for a matching set of lovebugs. Identical twin girls are the coolest.

Arden: No one cares about the ballooning I've suffered. All you're thinking about is buying stuff.

Perri: It's simply because I can't think of anything better than us getting to raise and indoctrinate two little identical Ardens.

Vanessa: It is indoctrination, right? That's what we'll be doing. And we are kind of going to be raising them. Sisterhood and all.

Perri: We'll let the guys be involved a little bit, but we'll teach the munchkins all of the important things ourselves.

Arden: Like how to be awesome?

Vanessa: Like how to be a good friend?

Perri: Like how to look out for your girlfriends?

Ella: Like how to respect your elders, learn from them, and then adopt their best traits?

Vanessa: *pats head of little sister* I'm so proud of you for being an excellent acolyte. Speaking of excellence, how is that man who was almost mine? *snort, snort*

Arden: As if. We all know Shaw was destined for Vanessa. Even if Perri had blinders on for, like, ever about that pairing.

Perri: Enough about my brother, aka Vanessa's HUSBAND. I want to hear about Ella . . . our protege. Tell us about Mr. Sullivan.

Ella: *grins wickedly* *enjoys my man* *makes plans to surprise him in new lingerie later*

Arden: Yay! I'm glad it's going so well.

Ella: Me too. I have Jamie's stepmom to thank. That schemer. :)

Perri: Hello? My scheming husband played a big role.

Vanessa: I will never forget how Derek earned his wings as my cupid.

Ella: And I am eminently grateful to him as well. Especially since I think Jamie's going to propose this weekend.

Vanessa: *squeals!*

Arden: *squeals again!*

Perri: *squeals louder!*

Vanessa: Why do you think it's going to be this weekend?

Ella: Things he's asked me, plans he's making for us to go away, a certain delighted secrecy in his eyes.

Vanessa: So you're not going to be surprised?

Ella: Oh, I'm going to act surprised. But it won't be an act when I'm over the moon and say yes. I want this more than I wanted a love like those in the love stories. Because that's what I think this will be.

* * *

That weekend

Vanessa: OMG! He asked and she said yes! Show us the ring.
Ella: *flashes stunning picture of gorgeous diamond ring!*

Arden: It's so beautiful. I'm crying at the sparkles.

Perri: It shines. Look how it shines like the sun! But confession: Arden is crying because she can't fit out the door. I'm over here trying to shove her out on account of contractions and Gabe being on shift, but we just want to say we love your ring and we're so happy for you, Ella.

Ella: Go, go, go! We want babies!!

From the guys...

Shaw: Up for a beer after work? It's on me. Since I owe you beers for the rest of my life.

Derek: You won't get any argument from me on that, but go ahead and tell me why you're going to be the purveyor of all my beers.

Gabe: I'd also like to be included in that beer-for-life gift.

Shaw: Seems Jamie proposed to my wife's little sister.

Derek: Dude, you have me to thank for so many things.

Shaw: That's why I'm thanking you. Because it just keeps getting better and better. You setting up Jamie and Ella gave me what I needed.

Gabe: Hey, Shaw, do you think Derek can try to get a job as a matchmaker? Maybe he could go connect with Miriam and the other ladies. I hear they've been quite busy. Hunter just moved in with Madeline.

Shaw: Aww, Derek would look so cute with a diaper and bow and arrow, don't you think?

Derek: You guys can mock me all you want, but I just scored beer for life.

Gabe: And I will gladly snag one of your brews. Holy shit. I got to jump. Arden went into labor.

* * *

Twenty-four hours later

Gabe: And I am now the father of two beautiful twin girls, and I couldn't be happier. My babies are perfect, and I love them madly. Look at these angels.

Derek: They're beautiful, man. I'm so damn happy for you guys. Perri is honking the horn right now and demanding I get my butt over to the hospital.

Shaw: Heading over there in a few with Vanessa. Can't wait to meet 'em.

Gabe: Just look for the happiest guy here.

Shaw: I think it's safe to say we all are. The happiest guys.

Please enjoy STRONG SUIT, a short story about Noah and Ginny from Birthday Suit! Available only in paperback here in NOBODY DOES IT BETTER!

From the day he meets her in the conference room, Noah has his sights set on Ginny. But he'll need to pull out all the stops to win her over in this delightful office romance novella from #1 NYT bestselling author Lauren Blakely!

This story is dedicated to Joe Arden and Erin Mallon. Their lively and clever performances of these characters in the Birthday Suit audiobook inspired me to write a short story for Ginny and Noah.

HER PROLOGUE

A year ago

For the record, I did not—underline *not*—make the offer because he's hot.

I *only* made the offer because I'm helpful.

That was it.

That was all.

It went down like this.

At the end of a department-head meeting, my boss popped in, introduced the new director of sales, then—because he had an unexpected meeting with a client—asked if someone wouldn't mind showing him around.

Wouldn't mind?

Ah, hell no.

Because Noah Rivera was easy on the eyes.

And had the best smile ever.

But wait. That's not why I stuck my hand in the air.

"I'll be happy to show him around," I offered.

I did it because I liked to help.

Always had, always would.

"Why, thank you very much for being my tour guide," Noah said as we walked down the hall and I showed him the food labs at our chocolate company.

"I like to wear all sorts of hats. Head of marketing, captain of the softball team, and chief tour guide."

He stopped in his tracks. "Whoa. Did you just say softball team?"

I laughed. "Yes. Is that a surprise?"

"No. It's just—could this day get any better? I love softball."

I nudged his elbow.

Wait, did I just nudge his elbow?

Must behave.

I tried to make light of it. "Then you really ought to join our team. We have a ton of fun playing with the other food companies in the city."

He shot me a quizzical look. "And you like sports leagues? Like, really like them?"

"Sure. My daughter's school is right near the park, so it works out perfectly. She'll meet me at

Central Park and work on homework during the games."

His eyes swept down to my hand. Was he hunting for a ring? Well, he wouldn't find one.

"That is so cool that you're into—I mean, that Heavenly has a softball team. I'm fired up to join."

I flashed him a smile. "And I'm fired up you want to join."

I gave him the rest of the tour, popping by to say hi to other key team members, saving the best for last.

When we reached the corporate cafeteria, I swept my arm out wide. "And the best part? Heavenly has fabulous food. Yummy soups and delicious salads, and all sorts of options if you're a vegetarian or gluten-free, or what have you."

He nodded appreciatively at the spread. "This is going to be perfect."

I glanced at my watch. It was twelve thirty.

"Want to get something to eat?"

He smiled brightly. "Is everyone here as friendly as you?"

I shrugged playfully. "We do have a great group of people. That's why I've been here for more than a decade." I lowered my voice to a conspiratorial whisper. "Not for nothing, they do call me Ambassador Ginny."

He offered a hand. "Have I mentioned what a pleasure it is to meet you, Ambassador Ginny?"

"And it's a pleasure to meet you, Noah."

See, I did all that because I'm helpful.

Not because I was totally perving on the hot new guy.

We sat down and had lunch together, and that's when I made the biggest mistake.

"Tell me more about you."

I learned he lived in Queens, a few blocks from his family, had dinner with his parents every Sunday, and liked to play soccer with his older sister's youngest son.

He was a freaking twenty-five-year-old family man.

Thanks, universe, for the temptation.

HIS PROLOGUE

Seconds Later

She was friendly. Outgoing. Liked softball. Could talk up a storm.

She was also sexy as hell.

Oh, and she had an Australian accent.

Nothing hotter in all the world.

It was official.

I was falling in love.

CHAPTER ONE

GINNY

Groan.

Epic groan.

Absolutely epic groan worthy of a meme.

What was I thinking?

It's a question I write in my idea notebook in big, blocky letters. Then, because I want to make sure I remember it, I do a 3-D outline of the block letters.

What were you thinking, self?

I can't lead him on. Even though, my God, he is one of the cutest men I have ever seen. Cute as in red-hot, want to jump him, sexy as sin. But he's a boy, that's what I have to remind myself.

He's twenty-freaking-five.

What the hell would I do with a twenty-five-year-old? What would we talk about?

The same things you have been talking about.

I tell that voice to shut up.

Because those arms, that face, that dusting of scruff. The whole picture of Noah Rivera is everything I shouldn't want.

You don't need a younger man.

I write it again.

And again.

And again.

I shift gears from my reminder, scrawling out my ideas for our next marketing campaign, repeating silently, *He's too young for me.*

That's the trouble.

I've always been drawn to younger guys, and they're always dangerous. They're not serious, they don't have their act together, they don't know how to take care of you. Even though I absolutely do not, in any way, shape, or form need a man to take care of me, I *do* need someone I don't have to mother.

I'm thirty-five and I have a ten-year-old daughter. I'm a single mom, and I've only ever been a single mom.

My daughter's father left me before she was born, and I raise her all by myself. That's why I don't need yet another young guy in my life, someone who can't compute what it's like to have responsibilities. After all, he's the man who has enough free time to train for marathons, play in the company softball league, do a kickass amazing job as the director of sales, *and* probably get a full night's rest too. He might be exceedingly excellent at playing the Uncle Noah role, but c'mon. As endearing as that is, it's not the same as actually having everyday responsibilities of the permanent kind. I have to remind myself of that every time I feel tempted.

My boss taps the door to my office. "Idea," he announces.

I turn around and wave at the man the other ladies call Mr. Tall, Dark, and Handsome. They might as well add "Unavailable" to his business card, because Leo wears unattainable like a cologne. Works for me, since we're friends and only ever will be buds. I have this crazy hunch he's still carrying a torch for a woman from his past, but he doesn't like to talk about mushy stuff, so I don't prod too much about the woman named Lulu. A woman I've noticed him looking at pictures of on his phone now and then. "Hey, Leo. What ideas are rattling around in that big old brain of yours?"

He strokes his chin. "What's rattling is this. The Big Chocolate Show is coming up soon." He wiggles his eyebrows. "Are you thinking what I'm thinking?"

I raise my hand like I have the answer in class. "That we're going to gorge ourselves on chocolate to successfully achieve the nirvana state known as a chocolate coma?"

He taps his skull. "You can indeed read my mind. Because I do fully expect us to sample as much as we possibly can."

I pat my stomach. "I'm in. I'm awesome at chocolate sampling. You ever need help with that, you call on me."

"You're the only one I would ever call on." He clears his throat. "But in all seriousness, what I was really thinking was at the show we should look for the next rising star."

I bounce on my toes at the prospect of finding a top chocolatier to design a line of craft chocolate for Heavenly. "Yes, that was actually the real mind meld that I was receiving from you. Brilliant idea, and I'm going to be on the lookout."

That's what I focus on this afternoon: devising a strategy for the upcoming trade show. I don't at all think about the young, sexy, muscular, perfect-bodied, Michael Peña look-alike who tried to make *an electric toothbrush is like a vibrator* joke.

I might, though, use one of those devices tonight while thinking about him—and it's definitely not the electric toothbrush.

The next day, in the break room, I find Noah digging into a kale salad.

That's a sign right there. I despise kale, and Noah likes it.

All I have to do is focus on things I dislike, and I'll get rid of my desire for him.

I mime gagging.

CHAPTER TWO
NOAH

I take the bait.

"Hmm. I get the feeling you're trying to say you don't like kale? Is that what you're saying, Ginmeister?"

She rolls her eyes. "Noah, no one likes kale."

I stand tall and proud in front of the podium in kale defense. "Not true. I love it, love it, love it. Like adore it. I think it's one of the greatest foods ever."

She shoots me a skeptical look. "That's not possible."

"No, it is possible. See?" I take another bite and I chew, smiling and humming as I go. Oh, that was a bit of a mistake, because kale definitely takes a couple of years to chew through, and that's going to make it harder for me to talk, and talking is absolutely one of my strong suits when it comes to Ginny.

Except it's also my wild card still, because what if I say something that turns her off? Screw it. I'm the eternal optimist, so I choose to believe everything will all be good. "I love kale, and I bet you can too."

"But you're a health nut," she says. "That means you have to love it."

"By virtue of being a card-carrying eater of veggies and protein?"

"Yes, you're a flag-waving member."

"Ha, you said 'member.'"

She laughs.

Like I said, the mouth is a wild card. "And kale is delicious."

"Maybe to someone who never eats chocolate," she suggests, her brow furrowing. God, she's adorable when she argues. She gets a little crinkle between her eyebrows that I want to run my finger over, that I want to press my lips against, that I want to kiss.

And I officially have it bad for this woman if the crinkle in her forehead gets me excited. "I bet you've never had a roasted sesame seed kale salad, have you?"

She pretends to wretch.

"How about kale mixed with brussels sprouts and lemon?"

She clutches her stomach. "Are you trying to make it sound as awful and miserable as possible?"

I laugh. "Ginny, you don't know what you're missing." *When it comes to kale and men.*

"I am definitely not missing kale."

I set down my salad bowl, reach for her arm, and wrap my hand around it. She's quiet at first, and so am I, because, hello, did I just kind of make a move by touching her arm? And does it actually feel better than how a hand wrapped around an arm should feel?

She lets her eyes drift to my palm, and I swear she trembles slightly, a little shudder that makes me think she likes it when I touch her. Makes me want to go for it with her. It emboldens me.

"Let me make you a kale treat," I say in my best sexy voice.

She smiles softly. Kind of sexy. A little sweet too. As I let go of her arm, her fingers trail down my wrist.

Holy kale smoothie, she *is* flirting with me, and I have a leafy vegetable to thank.

She pins her gaze on me, her eyes fierce, her expression playful. "Bring it on, Noah Rivera."

There. Right there. When a woman uses your full name, it's definitely a sign. A sign of something good.

So I keep it up. No need to stop the volley now. "And if I prove you like kale? What then? What happens if I win the great kale battle?"

"It's a contest?"

"Hell yeah. Contests are awesome."

She laughs. "Fine. If I win, you have to make my next PowerPoint."

I scoff. She probably thinks it's a punishment. Little does she know nothing gets me down, not even PowerPoints. I'm actually ridiculously good at them, and I tell her as much.

"Ginny, I'm the master of PowerPoints. You can count me in."

"The master of PowerPoints, you say? Tell me what other talents you have. Can you fold laundry?"

I puff out my chest. "I can fold laundry, I can do my own laundry. I'm fully house-trained," I pause, then add, "in chores."

"Stop, Noah, you're getting me excited." Excited is exactly where I want her.

"Chores get you excited?"

"Chores are the way to my heart."

I decide to nudge open that door, leaning on my sexiest voice. "Would you let me do some chores for you?"

She waves her hand in front of her chest, like she's heating up. "Please. You can't say such seductive things in the office," she whispers.

Then I kick the door, as if I'm doing just that. Seducing her. "Cleaning dishes. Mopping floors. Sweeping, dusting, even . . ." I pause, take a beat. "Vacuuming."

She lets out a gasp, like I've hit the jackpot.

Then she schools her expression. "Anyway, enough about chores. I do have to go back to my desk and I can't very well spend the whole afternoon thinking about *chores*, can I?"

This woman. Damn. I want her. "I don't see the problem with that. But what do I get if I win?"

She tilts her chin, like she's thinking. Her eyes flicker, the hint of a smile in them. "What do you want?"

I strip away the teasing for a split second, dead serious. "I think you know what I want."

She swallows, looks away, then back at me, vulnerability in her eyes. "I do." And her expression and tone shift once more to flirty. "How about you get the *satisfaction* of me liking kale?"

Now that, that is definitely flirting. And I'm fully satisfied.

That night, after I run ten miles and do a full circuit of weights at the gym, I research the best kale salads in New York City, because no way am I fucking this up by making it on my own.

The next morning, on the way to work, I stop at a gourmet shop that is purported to have an incredible kale salad with sesame.

At the office later, I find her in the cafeteria and offer it to her for lunch.

She arches a skeptical brow. "I won't like this."

"I know. You won't like it. You'll *love* it."

She takes a forkful, chews, then stares daggers at me. "You tricked me."

I smile. "No trickery."

"This is bloody delicious."

"I told you so."

"But there's no way you can top this."

"I so can."

"Why do you like healthy food so much? And exercise?"

"Why? Because I want to live a long, healthy life, have a couple kids, and be around to play soccer with their grandkids too. That's why."

Her eyes flicker with something new, something I haven't seen in them before. "Is that so?"

Her tone is a little less of the usual flirty and sarcastic. It's almost like it's been stripped bare.

"That is very much so."

Her friend Julie joins her, so I return to my table. But I decide to have some more fun with the redhead, since she seems to like it so much. I ask the guy next to me for a sheet of paper from his notebook and a pen. I write in the middle of the paper. Then I fold it, give it some wings, and send it to her at her table. I watch as it soars, landing gently on Ginny's tray of pasta.

She seems surprised at first, then she looks up and notices me. I shoot her a grin. She smiles right back, and it sure looks as if she digs that I sent her this. That I'm not an annoyance to her, that she's getting quite the little kick out of this strange flirtation.

When she unfolds the wings, she grins. That sexy kind of smile. A little bit wicked, a little bit mischievous, something that tells me that maybe there are tingles running through her body.

God knows I have way more than tingles—I've got a whole lot of lust rattling through me as I savor the view of Ginny Perretti opening my paper airplane and reading my note.

"Satisfaction is coming."

CHAPTER THREE

GINNY

I shouldn't have touched his arm in the break room.

But who can blame me?

The man is hella toned. His body is like a work of exercise art.

Honestly, though, that's not his biggest selling feature. I'd still like him if he was soft in the middle.

Noah Rivera piques my interest for many other reasons. His persistence. His oddball humor. His zest for, well, everything.

His big, crazy heart. My God, the man wants to have kids and grandkids, and wants to play with them.

This is not fair.

Still, I need to resist hot young things. I've been down this road before, and I don't know that I want to travel it again and take a chance at being left high and dry.

After I put my daughter to bed, I vow not to text him.

Don't respond to his paper airplane message.

That's what I've been trying to do all afternoon. All evening.

Don't respond, don't give in, don't do it.

Two hours of Netflix bingeing later, I'm still resisting him.

Though I have given in to my third glass of wine, turned on the scalding hot water in the tub, and run a bubble bath.

Calgon, take me away.

I sink down under the water with my phone on the ledge of the tub. One more sip of chardonnay.

I picture Noah. Wonder what he's up to. I linger on that word. *Satisfaction.* And as the water slip-slides around my naked body, I feel my resistance tiptoe out the door.

Ginny: Satisfaction is coming? You don't say. All from more kale?

Noah: It was delicious, wasn't it?

Ginny: I'll admit it was quite tasty. Just as I said earlier.

Noah: Wait till tomorrow. I'll have something even better for you.

Ginny: Something better, you say?

Noah: Does that pique your interest?

I put my phone down so I don't reply with something naughty like, say, *You pique all sorts of parts*.

Just to be safe, I set the phone on the bath mat so I'm not tempted. But as I sink under the water, I replay our flirtations, our break room bump-ins, the little touches, and the paper airplane.

My skin heats up, and it's not from the water in the tub. It's from the way he flirts with me, and from the way I like it more than I want to.

CHAPTER FOUR

NOAH

The next day, I do it again. I find another shop, and I bring her another kale treat. I hand it to her in the break room.

"What's this?" she asks, as if she can't possibly believe it could be food. She holds it between her fingers.

I adopt my most serious tone. "We call that chocolate-covered kale."

She coughs. "Seriously? Are you trying to turn me off?"

Ah, hell. I just can't resist. I step closer. "No, I'm trying to turn you on. Don't you get that by now?"

She doesn't say anything at first, and I freeze, worried I've crossed a line. But she dips a toe over it, whispering, "Are you?"

"I definitely am." I take a beat. "So, is it working?"

She holds up a thumb and forefinger. "A little."

And I can work with *a little*. I can definitely work with that. "Excellent."

"Just promise me you won't ever bring me a kale smoothie."

I raise my right hand. "I'm taking an oath. I'm not that cruel. But chocolate-covered kale is another story. Why don't you try it?"

She takes a bite, considering. "What do you know? I don't think that's half bad."

I pump a fist. "I knew I could convert you."

She arches a brow. "I'm not totally converted. Now, in the future if you want to spoil me, chocolate and wine are the way to go."

I pretend to type. "Filing that away."

Leo strolls by, and I straighten. So does Ginny, almost as if we've done something wrong, and we don't want the boss man to catch us.

I choose to take that as another good sign, so much that I drop off a square of chocolate on her desk before I leave. That night while I'm at the gym, she texts me.

Ginny: Now that was even better than the chocolate-covered kale.

Noah: Excellent. Did you finish all of it?

Ginny: I did finish it. I'm quite good at finishing.

Oh, that's definitely a dirty euphemism.

Noah: I'm quite good at finishing too.

Ginny: What are you good at finishing?

Noah: Whatever I set my mind to. I have excellent stamina. I've finished marathons. I've finished races. I can finish whatever I need to finish.

Ginny: I love finishing.

And I'm on fire. Because she is almost certainly, most definitely, 100 percent all but sexting with me.

Noah: What are you going to finish right now?

Ginny: I'm having a soak in the tub.

Noah: You're a mermaid, yowza. Do you have a bath bomb?

Ginny: I bow to the inventor of bath bombs.

Noah: Favorite kind?

Ginny: Honeysuckle.

Noah: Of course. And you smell like honeysuckle.

Ginny: You've been sniffing me?

No point lying now, so I tap out a reply as I climb the StairMaster.

Noah: Yes. You smell incredible. Your scent is the perfect finishing touch.

Ginny: All this talk of finishing reminds me that I ought to finish this bath.

Noah: And after that, will you finish other things?

Ginny: It seems possible.

I stare at the phone as I climb, sweat slinking down my brow. Holy shit. She's a dirty girl.

We've jumped from electric toothbrushes to kale to wine to bath dirty talk, and I want to go over to her place right now and get in the tub with her, and I don't even like baths. I mean, come on, baths are kind of dirty.

I'm a shower guy. But a bath with Ginny Perretti? Hell yeah.

CHAPTER FIVE

GINNY

The next day I bang my head against the desk.

Must. Stop. Flirting.

I absolutely must. What is wrong with me?

I can't believe I got that bawdy last night. I can't even blame the wine. Because I know better. I was supposed to focus on arguing with Noah, finding things I dislike, reasons we wouldn't work, and instead I flirted with him yet again. I write my mantra down in my notebook.

Must. Stop. Flirting.

But I don't follow my own commands.

I keep arguing with him, like when I see him in the break room over the next week, and we debate who the best Bond is.

I say Pierce Brosnan, he insists on Daniel Craig.

We discuss when mason jars became okay for

pretty much everything, and then we talk about murses. I don't mind them, but he says no man should ever carry one.

And he sends me more paper airplanes. Sometimes he writes funny words in them. Sometimes he'll suggest a random topic he wants to debate the next day—why does honey belong in mustard but not ketchup?—and other times his paper airplanes are a little flirty.

Every day, though, I find myself looking forward to these moments, and at the same time, I remind myself that getting involved with a young guy from work would be a huge mistake, and I don't have room to make any.

A few days later, I stop by my boss's office before I leave for the day. "I'm all ready for the show this weekend. We'll go searching for our star."

In a split second, he closes his laptop. For a moment I wonder if he was looking at pictures of that woman again. He turns his gaze away from the machine, and Leo leans back in his chair. "I have my treasure map. I'm ready."

I thrust a fist in the air. "We won't leave until we track him or her down."

"We will be victorious."

"Of course we will."

As luck would have it, we do find a promising prospect at the chocolate show, a lovely, friendly, wildly outgoing woman with crazy curly hair, bright blue shoes, and a big personality. I hit it off with her instantly then learn something extraordinary.

She extends a hand. "Lulu Diamond."

Ohhhhhhh.

Well.

That's rather interesting.

She's the woman from Leo's past.

She's the one I'd bet a lifetime of chocolate he still carries a torch for, even if he'd deny it under oath or severe tickling.

But requited or unrequited love isn't for me to weigh in on.

"Ginny Perretti. Pleasure to meet you."

She glances at my jewelry, a heart-shaped necklace my daughter gave me. "I love your necklace, and you have the best hair."

I pat my red locks. "And you're perfect. You're hired. For anything and everything."

"Excellent. I'll be there tomorrow morning at nine a.m. on the dot."

I decide I love her, and I'm pretty sure I want her to be my new best friend.

That's one more reason I'm glad my company chooses her as our next rising star chocolatier.

But the weird thing is, when I sit down for lunch at the cafeteria a few weeks later and see she's chatting with Noah at the salad bar, a small nugget of jealousy digs into me. I'm almost embarrassed that I'm the least bit envious.

I like Lulu. I consider her a fast friend, and I don't want to feel so green, especially since nothing has happened with Noah.

I remind myself that Noah's friendly, he talks to everybody. So when Lulu sits down with me to dine, I shove thoughts of him away once again.

That's truly becoming my top sport—denying my desire for the hot young guy who's become so much more than that. He's become the man I'm interested in. Very, very interested in. Because this hot young guy is so good, and honorable. It's not him, it's me—my past makes me want to be very, very cautious.

"I'm so glad it's you who's the rising star," I say.

"Well, I'm glad it's me too," she says.

"We need more chicks here at the office."

"Girl power. I'm all for that."

As we chat about her plans for the new line of chocolate, something whooshes over my head. A paper airplane lands in front of my tray, and a rush of heat spreads across my chest. "Noah," I say, rolling my eyes to deflect but unable to hold in a smile.

"Noah sends you paper airplanes?"

I pick up the winged object. "He likes to send these to me at lunch. He's such a goofball."

"Regularly? He sends them regularly?"

"Once or twice a week."

"Pretty sure that means he's into you."

I try to dismiss the idea, even though I know he is. But if I give in to it, I'll give into him. And it's too soon. "Oh, no. He's just . . . festive."

Lulu glances behind her, and Noah waves to me. "No. I think he has a thing for you. A big thing. The look on his face seems to say it all. What about you? Is it mutual?"

I've been storing all my worries inside me, and at last I have the chance to talk them through. I blurt out, "I'm thirty-five. I'm ten years older than he is. Is that terrible?"

"Only if you let it be terrible. But your face says you like him too."

My stomach swoops. What am I going to do about all these butterflies? What am I going to do about Noah?

I look over at him, taking in his handsome face, his golden skin, his dark hair, and his smile. I don't even want to admit it to myself, much less to her, but I think I need to.

"Maybe I do," I say, since the truth feels better.

"Maybe someday, then, for the two of you."

"Maybe someday," I echo.

After Lulu leaves, Noah walks over, clears his throat, and hands me a paper airplane.

This one seems different than all the others, but the trouble is I don't know if I'm ready yet to set aside my rules.

Even though I find myself wanting to more every day I spend around him.

CHAPTER SIX

NOAH

Do it now.

A voice in the back of my head repeats: *Do it now. Just go for it. Ask Ginny out this weekend. Ask her out for lunch. Ask her out for coffee. Ask her out for a glass of wine. Ask her to go bath-bomb shopping. Ask her out to go taste-test kale salad anywhere. Take your chance.*

This time I listen to the voice, writing on the paper airplane, then personally delivering it as we leave the cafeteria together.

She opens it as we walk, reading the words I wrote.

"Someday I'd like to take you out."

Her eyes meet mine, and hers seem to sparkle with a little bit of hope, maybe even possibility. "You would?"

I keep going for it. "I would. What would you say if I asked you?"

She nibbles on her lip, sighing. "I don't know."

That's when I remind myself that love is a marathon, it's not a sprint. I press my hand over hers. "Don't give me an answer now, then."

"Why do you say that?" she asks curiously.

"Because 'I don't know' isn't the answer I want."

A smile seems to sneak across her face. "What is the answer you want?"

"The *only* answer I want is yes."

Her smile stretches further. "And you think I'm going to give you a yes?"

"I'm an optimist. Optimism is my strong suit. Maybe even my strongest."

"That's a good strong suit to have."

"It is," I agree, since it's what's going to fuel me as I run this marathon with Ginny. "Now isn't the time. But someday it's going to be a yes."

"Someday you say?" She's smiling wider now.

"What do you think, Ginny?" I ask as we reach the stairwell. "Will it be someday?"

"Maybe," she says, and that's already better than "I don't know."

"Excellent. You think I can get you from a maybe to a yes soon?"

She shrugs, a little playfully. "I think maybe if you try hard enough, you just might do that."

"I can do that. I can definitely do that."

She dusts invisible lint off my shoulder. "Go for it, Noah Rivera. Wear me down."

The die has been cast, the gauntlet has been thrown, and I make it my mission to wear her down, but in, you know, a positive way, the way we both want.

The next week, as we embark on a crazy corporate scavenger hunt across New York, I work my magic.

She smiles.

She laughs.

We talk and talk and talk.

So much so that I'm confident I'm closer.

And one day, when I ask her out again, I'm pretty sure she'll say that someday is now.

For more on Noah and Ginny's burgeoning romance, read their story as it unfolds alongside Lulu and Leo's in *Birthday Suit*, available now on all retailers!

ALSO BY LAUREN BLAKELY

FULL PACKAGE, the #1 New York Times Bestselling romantic comedy!

BIG ROCK, the hit New York Times Bestselling standalone romantic comedy!

MISTER O, also a New York Times Bestselling standalone romantic comedy!

WELL HUNG, a New York Times Bestselling standalone romantic comedy!

JOY RIDE, a USA Today Bestselling standalone romantic comedy!

HARD WOOD, a USA Today Bestselling standalone romantic comedy!

THE SEXY ONE, a New York Times Bestselling bestselling standalone romance!

THE HOT ONE, a USA Today Bestselling bestselling standalone romance!

THE KNOCKED UP PLAN, a multi-week USA Today and Amazon Charts Bestselling bestselling standalone romance!

MOST VALUABLE PLAYBOY, a sexy multi-week USA Today Bestselling sports romance! And its companion sports romance, MOST LIKELY TO SCORE!

THE V CARD, a USA Today Bestselling sinfully sexy romantic comedy!

WANDERLUST, a USA Today Bestselling contemporary romance!

COME AS YOU ARE, a Wall Street Journal and multi-week USA Today Bestselling contemporary romance!

PART-TIME LOVER, a multi-week USA Today Bestselling contemporary romance!

UNBREAK MY HEART, an emotional second chance contemporary romance!

The Heartbreakers! The USA Today and WSJ Bestselling rock star series of standalone!

Unzipped, when the dating coach meets her match!

Birthday Suit! A USA Today Bestselling forbidden romance!

The New York Times and USA Today Bestselling Seductive Nights series including *Night After Night*, *After This Night*, and *One More Night*

And the two standalone romance novels in the Joy Delivered Duet, *Nights With Him* and Forbidden Nights, both New York Times and USA Today Bestsellers!

Sweet Sinful Nights, Sinful Desire, Sinful Longing and Sinful Love, the complete New York Times Bestselling high-heat romantic suspense series that spins off from Seductive Nights!

Playing With Her Heart, a USA Today bestseller, and a sexy Seductive Nights spin-off standalone! (Davis and Jill's romance)

21 Stolen Kisses, the USA Today Bestselling forbidden new adult romance!

Caught Up In Us, a New York Times and USA Today Bestseller! (Kat and Bryan's romance!)

Pretending He's Mine, a Barnes & Noble and iBooks Bestseller! (Reeve & Sutton's romance)

The Break Up Album, the USA Today Bestselling standalone romance! (Matthew and Jane's romance)

My USA Today bestselling No Regrets series that includes

The Thrill of It (Meet Harley and Trey)

and its sequel

Every Second With You

My New York Times and USA Today Bestselling Fighting Fire series that includes

Burn For Me (Smith and Jamie's romance!)

Melt for Him (Megan and Becker's romance!)

and *Consumed by You* (Travis and Cara's romance!)

The Sapphire Affair series...

The Sapphire Affair

The Sapphire Heist

Out of Bounds

A New York Times Bestselling sexy sports romance

The Only One

A second chance love story!

Stud Finder

A sexy, flirty romance!

CONTACT

I love hearing from readers! You can find me on Twitter at LaurenBlakely3, Instagram at LaurenBlakelyBooks, Facebook at LaurenBlakelyBooks, or online at LaurenBlakely.com. You can also email me at laurenblakelybooks@gmail.com

Made in the USA
Middletown, DE
27 April 2019